M. STILLMAN

In The Joshua Sea

Contents

1

Loomings

One evening in spring, a yucca moth flies into a Joshua tree's flower. Veering downward, she keeps her head steady because of the pollen tucked beneath her chin. She lands on an off-white petal that is the same color as her wings, somewhere between eggshell and seashell white. Barely visible in the moonlit efflorescence, she walks silently towards the blossom's center, where she turns around and backs into the flower's ovary. Her egg-laying organ, the ovipositor, pokes a tiny hole in one of the inner petals, piercing the veil. Into the ovary, she deposits about a half-dozen eggs, which will hatch as larvae in a few weeks.

But what will the larvae eat? The yucca moth still holds the pollen ball from another Joshua tree under her chin. When her ovipositor is at the flower's ovary, and her body is parallel to the style, her head is perfectly positioned to access the open stigma, the uppermost of the flower's female parts. With evolved precision, she inserts the pollen into the stigma. Now the flower is fertilized, so it will eventually transform itself into fruit with seeds that the hungry yucca moth larvae can consume. But the larvae will only eat a portion of the seeds, and the remaining ones will have a chance to grow into Joshua trees.

With her underchin free of pollen, this yucca moth shakes her head from side to side thrice in its range of motion. Then she flies twice the length of her half-inch body to the nearest pollen-rich anther at the tip of the stamen, one of the hermaphroditic flower's male parts. She gathers fresh pollen with her specialized mouth appendages that reach like sticky tentacles, taking some pollen from this anther, some from another. She forms it into a ball, and tucks it under her chin again.

Then she flies up and out in the moonlight to another pale blossom on another Joshua tree, attracted by the freshness of the pollen's fragrance, and sensing minimal visitation from other yucca moths. There, too, she will oviposit and pollinate, so that this flower can also produce the seeds that her larvae will eat in a few weeks. Then the larvae, in the form of tiny caterpillars, will burrow pinpoint holes through the fruit's husk and drop to the sand. They will dig a few inches into the ground, and spin cocoons in which they shelter for most of the year, or maybe several years. But a few weeks after the larvae drops, the fruit will also fall to the sand, where its seeds might grow new Joshua trees, or be dispersed by elements and animals to grow elsewhere in the desert. With their genesis, lifespan, and destinies intertwined, moth larvae and Joshua seeds will grow into their next phases of life, which are made possible by each other.

Joshua trees are not pollinated by breezes, bees, birds, butterflies, or bats. The yucca moth is the only agent that can pollinate the yucca family including the Joshua tree. Joshua seeds are the only food that the yucca moth larvae consume as they hatch from eggs that were placed into the Joshua flower in spring, when the blossoms open to receive moonlight and moths. The Joshua tree and yucca moth have co-evolved to be mutually interdependent, each species working to ensure the other's survival as much as their own.

2

Stowing Down & Clearing Up

"Too many variables," said Stan. He slid the combination square into his front pocket. "This isn't a concentric load. It's eccentric. The stresses come from every which way." He shrugged.

"You're sounding like a schoolbook again, professor," said Jem, smiling. "All we have to do is clear out the rotten timber and reinforce."

"Well, if we were doing this in an office, in a city, as engineers for a client, we might do a stress test on a model," said Stan. Jem gave him a dubious look. Stan continued, "It's pretty damn skewed." He put down his pencil in the light of the carbide lamp. They were in a 'drift' that branched horizontally from a vertical shaft, fifty feet below the surface of the desert.

"Skewed, huh? We're the ones who'll be skewed if we can't bring ore down that line tomorrow. The Captain has his plans."

"I haven't given up. I'm just making observations."

"Then how do we shore it up?" asked Jem.

"Same as we did on that other adit," replied the former engineering student. "Eyeball it and half-ass it."

Jem chuckled. He knew that their supports would hold up better than most of the mines in the Mojave.

A few yards from the top of the same mine shaft, an iguana tunneled through sand and below rock. Her subterranean path was nearly horizontal, a tangent from the surface at a slightly acute angle. The hole was a touch wider than her body with claws extended, and barely taller than her shoulders and spine, which she could contract toward flatness when necessary. She scooped with her claws, bringing sand up from the hole as she backed out scrunching. At the top, she pushed the sand aside with her tail, making a smooth path around the entrance. Buried in the sand pile was a rusty bottle cap, a tiny white seashell, and a rock that contained a fair amount of gold. The iguana felt the sun for a moment on her head, on her sand-and-shadow colored body, and on her patterned tail. Then she scrambled to the lip of the burrow and went back down, camouflaged to the point of disappearance.

Above the heads of the miners, above the head of the iguana, beyond the visible stars, a region of space/time absorbed all matter and energy including light, sound, and reason. Some called it a black hole. But that name could not convey or contain the active, almost intentional darkness, a sky-pulsing void that radiated entropy. The miners and the iguana could not see it, touch it, or know it. But on some level, they could sense it, and it was there.

3

The Line

In the afternoon shadows below a brittlebush, a bobcat was almost concealed. He watched three young antelope squirrels scamper a few yards away, foraging and nibbling, then chasing each other, and teasing the bobcat by running across his field of vision. Even if the bobcat were to pounce, they were quick and agile enough to change directions while he was in mid-air. The squirrels also knew that they could run from sunlight into shadow and back again, and the bobcat's eyes would need a second to adjust. One of the antelope squirrels sat in the sun, shading himself with his white tail, looking directly at the bobcat and challenging him to a playful chase.

Flat to the ground, the bobcat glanced at the antelope squirrels with his eyes half-closed and his tail twitching slightly. Unless one of them blundered and came within a paw's swipe, he wasn't interested. But he knew that larger, meatier animals were attracted to the same areas that appealed to the antelope squirrels. A covey of quail had stepped across the far side of the clearing, making their happy, squeaky sounds as they browsed for food. He had waited for them to come within the leaping range of his hiding spot, but they had turned towards the creosote. In this same place a week earlier, he had ambushed a roadrunner while it was stalking a sparrow, and he was hoping for a similar meal now.

As the antelope squirrels moved elliptically away from the bobcat, he napped for a few seconds as cats do, with eyes slightly open and aware even as he slept. He suddenly opened his eyes fully when he saw movement on the plateau below. His ears raised, and he turned his head receptively. He had been seeing humans more often on the mountainside, near a couple of shacks and a deep hole in the ground. Humans weren't prey for him, and they usually weren't predators either, though one had shot at him with a rifle a couple of years earlier. The bobcat observed the human creatures carefully, as they were a special case in the animal kingdom. They walked strangely on their hind legs, and did things that other animals were unlikely to do. They frequently did things that other animals would refuse to do.

The motion he saw was a man, who had been sitting on a stool, standing up, but not gracefully. He held a tobacco pipe in his hand, which the bobcat hadn't sensed because it was downwind. The man was looking across the *playa*, his eyes shaded by the bill of a cap. When he put the pipe in his vest pocket and took a few steps, the bobcat noticed that he had a limp. It was then that the bobcat remembered seeing the same man in the same place a few days earlier.

Then the bobcat saw another man approach the plateau from below. He was younger and more spry than the first man, and his climb was sure-footed and direct. The man in the cap watched him approach, and the other man held his hands open and away from his sides. Then he waved one hand in greeting, and said some words that were carried away by the wind.

The man in the cap replied, the other man nodded pleasantly, and they shook hands. The man in the cap held his palm up towards a pair of wooden chairs, and they sat down to talk. The bobcat, watching from above, drifted back into sleep, with his eyes mostly closed, his ears relaxed, and his nose in some brittlebush blossoms that had fallen.

Haberman took the pipe out of his vest pocket, and inspected it. There was still some unburned tobacco in the meerschaum bowl. "I've been told you have some mining experience, William."

William Quine nodded and replied, "Yes, I worked last summer near Corona, crushing and loading ore, and doing odd jobs at the mill. Busy place, ten stamps."

"I know that mill. What other mining have you done?"

"I did some panning for gold in the Whitewater when I was a kid."

Haberman stirred the pipe tobacco with an implement that swiveled from his pocket knife. "The mining in these mountains is between those two extremes, and a little different. Nobody pans for gold around here, because there's not enough water, and not much placer gold left. But this job won't be just hauling and crushing ore like you did at Corona. That would be part of it though. Everybody on the crew will be doing most every job eventually."

Quine looked at the dilapidated shacks and the old head frame over the shaft. "I'd imagine you'd scale up if you struck a nice lode."

"That's right," said Haberman, nodding. "I'm looking to run a four-man crew at first. A couple of young fellows are working in a drift down the shaft right now. Timbering, mucking, and blasting."

The conversation paused for a couple seconds while they both watched a red-tailed hawk, flying at altitude towards the peaks.

"I remember the Anaconda Mine from years ago," said Quine.

"My lease started about three weeks ago, on the first of March. It hasn't been active in a while."

"I think people were working it in my grandfather's day. Is there any gold left?"

"Oh, I have some ideas. Did you grow up around here?"

"My grandparents lived in Twentynine Palms, near the oasis. I stayed there a couple summers when I was a kid, and now I'm living in town."

"Were they Chemehuevi?" asked Haberman.

"Chemehuevi and Serrano," replied Quine. "My father's side was English, German, probably others."

"I've worked with some good people who were called *'mestizo'* and so forth, but I called them by their rightful names," said Haberman.

Quine was uncomfortable with the topic. He had been called "half-breed" and other names in the past. Haberman looked at the bowl of his pipe, and then spoke again.

"Do you remember if anyone was working this mine back then?"

"I drove down that road a few times, and hiked around here once, but it didn't look active," replied Quine.

"We've done some repairs, and cleaning up. There weren't too many bats or rats," Haberman joked.

"How about cats?" Quine smiled.

"Big cats that leave tracks. They know to be careful with that shaft right there," he gestured, "a couple hundred feet deep."

"I wonder why they went so deep. How about a new drift that might cross a vein?"

"That's what I'm thinking. But if this mine doesn't pay, I have some other claims near here. This is still gold country," he said confidently.

Quine cleared his throat. "What are you looking to pay at first, Captain, if you don't mind my asking?"

"Three dollars a day for now, but if we strike a rich vein here or at one of the claims, I'll form a mining company and grant shares to the most loyal employees. Then you'd get a percentage of the profit, whatever it is, and it could be bountiful."

Quine nodded and remained silent for a moment, thinking. He contributed twenty dollars a month for the group house in Twentynine Palms, but would like to contribute a little more. Would his '25 Ford make it back and forth every day? Some of the wiring was questionable, and the tires had all been patched at least once. But with this job, he might be able to afford a better car after a few months.

"Did you go to school around here, William?"

"I went to the Sherman Institute, sir." He paused for a moment. "What you might call an Indian School. I also attended some classes at the college in Riverside."

Haberman nodded. He respected education, though his own was informal and self-directed. "I fought alongside some Sherman braves in the war. Good men. What did you do after that?"

"I was in the Navy from '26 to '28. Honorable discharge."

Haberman grinned. "Navy man! I spent ten years in the

Navy, right up to the armistice."

Quine straightened in his chair as if to stand and salute, then just saluted. "Thank you for your wartime service, sir. Were you a Captain in the navy?"

"No, no. At ease, young man. I was the Chief Boatswain of my last ship, the *U.S.S. Lampkin*. But let's talk about the job at hand. You look like you're about 25 years old?"

"I'm 27," replied Quine.

"Very good. I'd like you to take a test."

Haberman reached into a wooden crate next to his chair, pulled out a short length of rope, and tossed the line to Quine.

"Can you tie a bowline knot?"

Quine smiled. He grasped the rope a couple inches below its end, and held it up with his right hand. Then he reached the rope behind his back, looking at the sky while he blindly and single-handedly made the loop, manipulated the end through it, then around and through the loop again, and then cinched it with a tug. He brought the knot from behind his back and presented it matter-of-factly to the Captain.

Haberman smiled. "Oh, you're a Navy man all right. Yesterday I used a bowline to lower a tool bag into the shaft, and used it for lots of other things over the years. Handiest knot there is."

"I tied a bowline through the clew of a jib a few times. Most of my hitch was on steamships, but we did some sailing too, especially during training."

The conversation paused for a couple seconds as they each remembered sailing days, and the tranquility of a sailboat in calm water with a light breeze. Each had more than one reason for venturing to the Mojave, but both had noticed how the desert and sea, with their vast expanses and silent depths, touched human souls with a like power. Each had felt it on a level beyond the conscious mind and its paintbox of specific words, and now the feeling returned for a moment that invoked the same power of silence. Quine was most comfortable with a conversational rhythm that included rests, time to reflect and observe. But then Haberman remembered that he was interviewing a candidate for employment, and needed to take charge in a businesslike manner. He had some other questions in mind, but decided he wouldn't need them.

"Well, Mr. Quine," he said with a smile, "can you start tomorrow?"

"That would be great, Captain," replied Quine. "And you can call me William if you'd like."

"Good to have you with us, William. You can call me Joe if you want, but most everyone seems to call me Captain."

Quine glanced at Haberman's cap. It was a black cap of heavy waxed cloth that was similar to a sea Captain's hat, but with no insignia of any kind. "Thank you, Captain."

"Would you have time to help me with a little project right now? It's like tying a jib sheet to a clew."

"Sure."

"About a quarter-mile over that ridge is a stone cabin. It has a level floor, and I brought in a few cots, but we need to work on the roof."

"Is the lodging included with the job?"

"Yes, the cabin came with the mine lease. It hadn't been used in years, but we've been working on it. I slept there last night."

"I have a place to stay in Twentynine, but it would be good to have another option. Should we drive there?" asked Quine, thinking of Haberman's damaged leg, which had been obvious even with a couple steps.

"Yes, I have something to take over there. It's a pleasant little hike, but let's use my truck."

Quine nodded and rose to his feet. Haberman stood more slowly, and they started walking down the ridge to where his Ford Model A truck was parked on the sandy plain below. Haberman favored his left leg, taking shorter, safer steps with that side of his body. Quine patiently moved alongside him, subtly watching and ready to assist if necessary, but Haberman negotiated the sand and rock slope effectively despite his disability. When they were more than halfway to the car, Haberman stepped onto a flat rock that tilted slightly. He lurched and almost fell, then grabbed onto a large boulder to stabilize himself. Quine reached out to brace him, but Haberman scowled and almost slapped his hand away.

"Keep your hands off me! I don't need anyone's help."

Quine was taken aback. "I know you're able, Captain. I was just giving you a hand, like you'd do for me if I slipped."

Haberman grunted ambiguously, and they walked in silence to the truck.

A few miles away, in a place the two of them had never been, quartz sparkled in granite. From the east, west, north, and south, there had long ago steamed hot rivulets of quartz, feldspar, and gold, which cooled and brittled through the aeons. Denser than the granite that surrounded them, the veins had bisected ridges like white-hot knives, and sliced some of the boulders into rolling hemispheres. Four veins of quartz converged at this place, and paralleled at length until they submerged into the slow tides of the desert.

They drove around the line of monzogranite hills to a meadowed flatland that was surrounded by mountains on three sides. Among scattered wildflowers stood the knee-high remains of a small stone building that had fallen next to the walls of a stone cabin that stood intact.

"I wasn't sure if these buildings were part of the lease or not, but then I saw the letter on the cornerstones." Haberman pointed to a capital 'A' that had been scratched on the visible corners of the bunkhouse. Quine saw that it was also on one of the collapsed building's stones, which capped a pile of rubble like a child's building block.

Quine walked up to the stone bunkhouse and looked it over. All four walls were intact, with some gaps for windows, and a door that was on the opposite wall from the stone and brick fireplace, which contained recent ashes below a rack that held fresh wood. Most of the floor was natural bedrock that was flat and level, and the rest was flagstones embedded and aligned. The floor had been recently swept. There were a few cots folded and stacked against a wall, and a worn table under the window on the other wall. But there was no roof other than the bare ridge beam that spanned the apex.

Haberman saw Quine examining the beam, and said, "That's a replacement. The original roof burned up a long time ago." There were scorched stones and charred timber at the top of the walls. "But I brought what we need." He stepped to his truck and dropped the gate. "Can you help me with this?"

Quine walked over, and saw a folded piece of heavy canvas with grommets at the edge. He picked up one end at the same time that Haberman picked up the other, and they carried it over to the bunkhouse and sat it down.

"A sailmaker in San Diego cut this for me," said Haberman. "The cabin is sixteen by twenty-four, and this will overlap by a foot on each side." Quine looked at the top of the walls, and saw metal hooks embedded in concrete at each corner of the bunkhouse. Haberman continued, "We can secure the corner grommets with those hooks, and then run some guy lines through the other grommets down to long stakes."

"I lived in a tent cabin for a few weeks on an island in Hawaiian territory, but it didn't have a fireplace or a stone floor like this one."

"I had no complaints about tent cabins unless it was raining or hailing, and that doesn't happen much around here. Do you think you could reach the top of that wall if you stood on the window frame?" asked Haberman.

"Yes," said Quine, looking it over. "I could climb up on the edge if necessary too."

"Good, because we only have one ladder. I can be on the far side, standing on that." He started unfolding the canvas. "We can roll this up the long way, lift it to the edge of the roof, and hook it onto this side. Then we can unfurl the canvas over the top with a rope stretched across, and let it unroll itself down the other side."

They spent several minutes installing and securing the canvas roof, and attaching the guy lines to tent stakes with bowline knots. Haberman observed that Quine was a steady and efficient worker, and a nimble climber. Quine tried to keep an eye on Haberman at the ladder, and he noticed that on every other rung, the Captain was a little slower, pulling himself up with bulging arms. When they were finished, they walked inside and looked at the new roof, translucent in the afternoon sun.

"This is a good cabin, Captain," remarked Quine. It compared favorably to most of the shanties he had seen in the mining areas of Corona, Old Dale, and Music Valley.

"It's coming along. I'll have to figure out something for the windows, but this is livable." He looked around approvingly, and said, "Thank you, William. It will be good to work with you."

"Likewise, sir. What time should I be here tomorrow?"

"We'll start at seven a.m."

They shook hands, and Quine hiked over the ridge to where his car was parked by the mine. Haberman began cutting some canvas to shade the windows of the tent cabin.

4

The First Lowering

William Quine arrived at the Anaconda Mine a few minutes before seven the next morning, about an hour after the sun had risen over the mountains. As he walked up the slope, he saw the Captain and two other men sitting on the old wooden chairs near the outbuildings. They stood as he approached, and Quine guessed the two to be in their early twenties, a few years younger than himself, and a couple decades younger than the Captain.

"Good morning, William," said Captain Haberman. "These fellas are Jem Parker and Leif Stanicek." Jem was stocky and dark-haired, with a young man's freckles but a serious look on his face, wearing denim overalls. Leif was taller, with reddish blond hair parted on the side, wearing glasses and an expression of inner amusement. To Quine, they seemed younger than most of the miners he had encountered lately, and cleaner in appearance.

"Glad to meet you, William," said Jem Parker, reaching and clasping Quine's hand with a firm handshake.

Leif Stanicek said, "Hello, William. Most people call me

Stan."

"Good to meet you fellows. Looking forward to working with you," replied Quine as he shook hands with Stan.

"Looking forward to striking a motherlode," said Stan with a grin and a nod.

Quine smiled. "If it's here, let's find it." But he had mixed feelings about gold. His Native ancestors had revered quartz and turquoise, not gold. He knew little about the European-American side of his family, but had heard his father called a 'wildcatter,' a miner who traveled extensively, mostly solo, finding a small lode, working it to exhaustion, then moving on to the next. Though Quine did not articulate his thoughts to anyone but himself at the moment, he was returning to the desert to better understand both sides of his heritage. Could he ally their strengths within himself? Or could they be alloyed, like copper and tin to make bronze? He didn't know if that was even what he wanted, or if it would be a good thing. Or maybe they couldn't alloy, but had to stay separate in layers, like the two-toned rocks of the fire ring a few feet away.

Quine didn't get a gleam in his eye when gold was mentioned, like some he had known. But demand for gold had risen when the stock market and banks collapsed, and it became worthwhile to reopen some old mines. Like many others these days, he needed a way to make a living when some of the old ways had vanished. Anyone could get started in mining with a rock hammer and a claim form, or by banding together with others in a small mining company.

"Even though you fellas don't have a lot of mining experience, you each have skills and talents that can help us," remarked Haberman. "Jem was a farmer in Texas, and he's a good engine and tractor mechanic. Stan was studying to be an engineer in Chicago, he's worked on construction projects, and he's related to plumbers. William has been in the Navy, done some gold mining, can climb like a cat, and some of his people were in this desert thousands of years before the rest of us." The three of them mostly smiled at the Captain's summaries, which seemed terse and somewhat random but not inaccurate.

"I'll tell you more about myself later, but some of you already know that I was on ship during the war, and I saw some action that knocked me around a bit. I ended up in Twentynine Palms on Doctor Luckie's suggestion. Started mining, and I've made a living every year since, with help from my disability pension. Yes, they say I'm disabled, though I get around pretty well, considering. Sometimes I'm a little slow to climb a ladder or a steep slope. But I can skedaddle down a tunnel following the gleam of gold as well as anybody." Haberman looked around at them fiercely, his eyes bright under unruly eyebrows.

"I have the Anaconda lease for about eleven more months, with an option. We'll see what we can do with it. We should aim to bring up at least a half-ounce of gold in every ton of ore, and we need to process a couple tons a day. Ry Keane charges five dollars a ton to mill the ore. If we can't make our production target, we'll have to consider other mines and maybe some claims."

He took a step to the side unsteadily, his eyes on the horizon, then continued. "Four is the perfect number for a small mining company. There are a lot of jobs that require two-man teams, and it's safer to work in pairs. One team can be down below while the other is working on surface or transporting ore, and then trade off. I'll work with William today, he's the new fella. Stan and Jem, keep drilling on that rock face from yesterday, and muck out that sandy pocket. Let us know before you dynamite. Mr. Quine and I will be down there too, at the other drift that branches south. Let's go on down and get to work, gents." It was a miners' tradition to call each other 'gents,' mostly because other people didn't.

The miners spent the morning underground, hammering, drilling, and blasting, then mucking and loading. Percussive sounds traveled up the shaft, and could be heard at the head frame and beyond the fire ring. The sounds of metal against rock, accompanied by the vocal calls of humans seeking gold, had not been heard during the lifetimes of most of the local animals.

Some of the rocks on the surface, including the ones that formed the fire ring, were of a different composition than the monzogranite mountains that defined the horizons. These striated and variegated rocks, the most senior of any objects in the vicinity, were formed and strewn in the Pre-Cambrian era almost two billion years past. Geologists named them 'Pinto Gneiss' for the Pinto Basin, several miles down the road from the mine. The darker striations, made of dense, volcanic materials like iron, told of ignescent birth and magmatic upheaval. The light-colored bands, also lighter in weight, contained granite, quartz, and silicate materials that had folded into the mixture as it cooled and solidified before extrusion.

On a gneiss chunk near the mine shaft stood a mockingbird, camouflaged in gray, black, and white. He spent a long minute listening to hammers banging, loud talking, exertion and exhortation, and a muffled explosion. Obviously humans. He cocked his head to the left and the right, listening for a sound with character and regularity that could be usefully imitated. But he didn't like anything he heard, so he flew away.

Scooping and loading, Stan and Jem shoveled sand and pebbles from the horizontal drift into a wheelbarrow and the carts, which experienced miners called "mucking." By removing this pocket of sand, they could reach the more promising rock just a few feet away.

"Asphyxiation," declared Jem.

"That's one," answered Stan. "Also cave-ins."

Jem shoveled and then paused to say, "Snake bites."

"Didn't see many snakes in Chicago. Only the human kind."

Jem nodded. "We had 'em in Texas, but they were different kinds than you see here."

"I've heard about that Mojave Rattlesnake. Sometimes green, sometimes not. Maybe the worst."

"I was talking with Ned about those. They have two kinds of poison. One poison will paralyze their prey, while the other rots the flesh. Turns black and purple."

"Heard about that too. When they strike a person, within a few minutes they'll have trouble talking."

"Where I come from in Texas, we had copperheads, water moccasins, and coral snakes that you don't find here, and different kinds of rattlers. But they weren't as deadly as that Mojave green rattlesnake."

"They talk about sidewinders here too. They're not too big, but they curl in the sand, and you can't see 'em 'til you step on 'em."

"A few more kinds of rattlers too. Speckled rattlesnakes, diamondbacks, king snakes that kill other rattlers."

"No anacondas though," said Stan.

Jem smiled. "There are probably some other rattlers that we don't know about."

"And I hope we don't find out anytime soon," replied Stan.

"A few other ways to die. Exposure, thirst."

"Sunstroke. People freeze to death too, at night in the mountains if you're at altitude."

"Flash floods down canyons and washes," mentioned Jem. "Or a mine shaft might fill up with water."

"When it rains, it rains hard. Some of the roads become rivers, flowing fast."

"I heard about a mule team that got buried to their ears in wet sand, right on the highway." Jem scooped a shovelful of sand, and imagined a mass of it overtaking a team of mules, their nostrils flaring and ears flattening back in fear.

"Twentynine Palms Road goes through a low, flat part of the basin," said Stan. "That's why it's mostly straight instead of winding, like all the mountain roads."

"What about tarantulas and scorpions?"

"I don't think you die from those. But they'd probably hurt so much that they'd distract you from whatever you planned that day."

"Black widow spiders," declared Jem.

"Sure, they're here, in many a cabin corner. Can be fatal, usually not."

"What about coyotes? Mountain lions? Bobcats? Black bears?"

"They say it's rare for any of them to attack a human," said Stan.

"But would you smart talk 'em? Maybe explain some science?" asked Jem.

Stan almost kept a straight face but started to laugh. "Nope."

"How 'bout poisonous plants? Jimson weed for one."

"Yeah, maybe milkweed too," answered Stan. "What if you fell into a cholla patch?"

"You probably wouldn't die from that, especially if you got help," speculated Jem. "Other ways to fall to death though. Down a mine shaft, or down a mountainside."

"Yep," said Stan, stopping to stretch his tall frame. "Many ways to die, but very few ways to make a living."

"So how did an engineering student like you end up in the Mojave Desert? Where there's no college in the whole county?" asked Jem with a little smile that was visible in the light of the carbide lamps.

"I might ask you a similar question," replied Stan. "You're a farmer in a place where it's really hard to farm."

"Well . . ." said Jem, drawing out the word. They looked at each other and chuckled.

Jem put down his shovel, and reached into his bib overalls for the packet of chewing tobacco. Stan pulled down the bandanna from over his nose to his chin, and took a sip from his canteen. They blinked a few times, feeling the dust in their eyes. They had learned to take regular breaks to let the dust settle.

5

Knights and Squires

The four miners climbed in succession from the narrow shaft. The Captain was last and slowest. They blinked in the mid-day sun and stretched their limbs as if they were waking in the morning. Their lunches were in a cool metal chest that had been buried below a shaded rock on the hillside. They each took their lunch bag or box and went four separate ways to eat. After the first week, Captain Haberman had suggested that they eat lunch separately on days they worked together. Restricted to a narrow shaft or tunnel for hours, breathing the same stale air, each usually wanted a little sunshine and solitude during lunch hour. When each man finished eating, he could smoke, read, or take a brief siesta in the moderate springtime weather. They also spent time together in the tent cabin, but there had been only one evening when all four slept there, in the four separate corners, but spending almost twenty-four hours of the day together. A solitary lunch was welcomed by them all.

Haberman would sometimes talk of co-workers past, hungover miners or sailors who would sleep the whole break from lunch bell to work bell, paying the toll of larks and sprees that with habit, in his telling, became deadly sins. His favorite anecdotes involved unheeded warnings and unforeseen consequences. Don't have to worry about that tomfoolery with this crew, he told himself. The depression and calamities have brought a better class of man to the desert.

Today, he commandeered a shady, flat spot on a knee-high boulder, where he could see across the valley floor below. He unwrapped a semi-circular piece of cornbread that he had cut from a skillet-shaped loaf a couple of days earlier. As he chewed the bread, he wished he had some honey or jelly to spread on it, or some gravy to dip, anything to counteract the dryness. He took another swig of water from the canteen.

The valley stretched into the distance like a calm sea on a clear day. There were creosote bushes young and old, some brittlebush, acacia, yucca, and wildflowers blooming. Granite boulders stood in huddled groups and as staunch monoliths. The altitude was slightly below the level where Joshua trees would grow, but they were plentiful just a couple miles south. After being underground all morning, looking at rock a couple feet away, it was relaxing for his eyes to focus on more distant objects. But today his gaze retracted to several dragonflies diving and hovering from shade to sunlight, landing on nearby bushes, seemingly looking at him with curiosity. Haberman was amused to see them. "Little dragons! How did you hatch so far from water? Did your mother find a rainwater hole? Did a little cloud burst over your heads?"

He looked at the nearest dragonfly, and its compound eyes seemed to be looking back at him. The shape of the dragonfly's head, with its bulging eyes, reminded him of a hammerhead shark. He saw the dragonflies as little sharks darting through an ocean of air, smelling the blood cargo of mosquitoes and drawn to them. Whenever he noticed dragonflies diving for prey, he rooted for the dragonflies, sometimes vocally. On a Navy ship, decades earlier, while up in the crow's nest with binoculars, he had seen a giant cluster of dragonflies migrating across the Indian Ocean, hundreds of miles from fresh water. They had been at his eye level, a few feet away, and seemed to change course slightly to avoid the ship. When he was a boy, he had associated dragonflies with streams and ponds, but as he traveled through the years, he was impressed to find them over the ocean and in the desert, seemingly everywhere. He admired their tenacity and adaptability as much as their ferocity.

After finishing his cornbread, Haberman reached into his lunch pail for the can of sardines he had packed. He turned over the can and detached the key. Then he inserted the can's lid flap into the key slot, and turned the key a few times to scroll the lid open. He detached the key and used its handle to pry out a couple of sardines, which he ate gladly. The cornbread/sardine combination was one of his regular lunches, and he felt fortunate for that, because too many people were surviving on worse.

Stan stepped around a rocky promontory to a level area with some dappled shade. He sat on a boulder that was shaped like a tree stump, then reached into his lunch sack. He took out a can of baked beans and a can opener tool, which he used to pierce the lid and circumratchet the top. Then he took out a small can labeled "cocktail wieners" and opened it the same way. He had purchased a case of the wieners at the factory in Chicago, and brought them west in the trunk of his Studebaker. They had been a convenient meal when not much else was available or affordable, but he had grown tired of them. He combined them with the beans in the simplest of recipes, and ate them cold. It wasn't his best or favorite lunch, but it worked.

Dragonflies were flitting about the area. He watched one in its flight, and tried to study the double pair of wings as they flapped and stabilized. Da Vinci's drawings of a hovercraft came to mind. Leonardo had studied the dragonfly to learn its aeronautics. Stan watched one halt in mid-air, and then zoom off in a different direction. Another hovered in place, seeming to consider more than one course of action, like a person at a fork in the road. A few years earlier, Stan had seen an experimental helicopter at Grant Park in Chicago. He was intrigued by its coaxial system of rotors, with concentric shafts turning independent pairs of blades. But its brief demonstration of lift and yaw seemed clumsy and lurching when compared to the grace and precision of the dragonfly.

After he finished the pork and beans, he took another sip of water from the canteen, then spent some time stretching his legs. The mine felt cramped to him most of the time, and he savored the fresh air and sunlight. Stan knew that he didn't want to work underground for many more years, certainly not the rest of his life. But gold mining was a grand pursuit that could be ventured with little cash in hard times, and maybe if they worked hard, they could get lucky.

Sitting with his back against a flat-sided boulder, Jem reached into his lunch box for a baloney sandwich. He folded down two corners of the waxed paper and took a bite. Then he reached for the bottle of orange soda, and used the opener from his pocket knife. The soda was still a little cold from the icebox at the store in Twentynine Palms that morning, and it had helped cool the sandwich as outdoor temperatures warmed to seventy-five degrees by noon. It was a pleasant day in the desert, like many in the spring. He liked this shaded ledge a little higher in the hills. The greenery made him think of his Texas hometown, west of Austin where the hill country started.

Some people said that town was one of the greenest in the state of Texas, with springs, rivers, creeks, and a healthy aquifer. To Jem, it had been a good place to grow up, fishing, exploring, playing baseball. But just as he reached the age when he wanted to start working hard for a living, the economy collapsed. The most fertile farmland in the area was owned by a handful of fortunate families, or absentee landlords in Dallas or Houston. Much of the rest went for ranching and cattle grazing. When hard times started, those who sharecropped or leased land had the hardest time of all, especially the younger people just getting started. Jem had tried to farm for a couple seasons on dry land that he subleased from other people who had given up. He had worked hard on those craggy hillsides, with their uncertain terraces and plow-chipping pebbles. He tried corn and wheat, then sorghum, but none of them yielded enough to make it worthwhile, especially during drought. His view across the valley as he labored had been thousands of more arable acres owned by other people, but they weren't doing so well now either.

In '30 and '31, banks failed and commodity prices sank. The drought continued through another season and then the next, and then another. The losses compounded more quickly than the gains ever had. As an occupation, farming became what they called "a tough go," even if you had good land and could access water. Many from his generation had left town, some for military service, others to try their luck in other places and in other fields.

Jem's main asset was a five-year old Ford truck that ran well, so he decided to take advantage of the mobility. He gave up his rented shack and unyielding land in Texas, and said goodbye to his relatives, friends, and the gal that he had been seeing every now and then. He packed a tent, some food, water, and a few tools, and drove west to the golden state, with mostly good weather and good roads, but slow with likewise traffic. Extended families with in-laws and cousins in caravans and convoys were fleeing the Dust Bowl and hard times. It seemed like every few miles there was a "Hooverville," a shantytown of the unemployed and destitute who wouldn't be voting for their camp's namesake in the upcoming election. An old miner at one of the Hoovervilles had told him, "A strong young fellow like you could do well around Twentynine Palms, it's a growing town," and based on nothing more than that, he decided to give it a try.

Eight weeks had passed quickly. With odd jobs in town and then mining, Jem had worked his way to a basic solvency, and now he felt like he had prospects for something closer to prosperity, despite the hard times. He finished his sandwich and took another sip of orange soda, then put the bottle down on a flat slab of bedrock.

There were still a few minutes before he would hike down the wash and go back to the mine. He took out a pouch of tobacco and rolled a cigarette. He most frequently chewed from a different pouch, but he sometimes smoked. As he moistened the gum edge with his tongue, he looked up and noticed a dragonfly sitting on a creosote branch a couple of feet away. It slowly raised and lowered its wings, then sat motionless.

When Jem was a boy, he and his fishing buddies figured out quickly that dragonflies wouldn't sting, and then they started to like them. If one landed on your fishing pole, they told each other, it meant you were about to catch a fish. If you didn't catch a fish, well, you must have done something wrong. This dragonfly's metallic-looking segments, glinting silvery blue in the sunlight, reminded Jem of a knight's armor. The ability to turn at right angles with a zig-zag was like the knight's movement in chess. None of the other chess pieces could zig or zag, not even the powerful queen. Like the knight, the dragonfly's maneuverability distinguished it from other creatures on life's chessboard, and maneuverability was a useful skill when life took a turn. Jem spent a few restful minutes smoking and watching the dragonflies.

William Quine walked up a wash that deepened into a canyon, and he passed the petroglyph that drew his interest to this *arroyo* weeks earlier. The glyph looked like a plus sign or cross that abraded a granite boulder, low to the ground at knee level. He understood the cross to represent a dragonfly and its wings. Since dragonflies needed fresh water, it usually meant there was a tank, dam, natural trough, or spring in the area. Even in places where the spring had gone dry, or a tank had filled with sand, there might still be ancient glyphs. Sometimes these places had grinding *morteros* of various sizes, some deep enough to hold rain water for several days. After a hundred feet of ascension, he detoured into a side canyon that branched off to the left.

He looked to a certain landmark, a rock with the oldest known style of petroglyphs, called 'cupules' by English-speaking anthropologists. The rock was a short climb ahead, its granite face angled obliquely but still able to communicate information like a road sign. Though partly obscured by a bladderpod bush that had grown up in recent decades, now blooming yellow, he saw the boulder's rows of round indentations, spaced regularly on the outward-facing plane. He had been told that the cupules were carved at least a thousand years earlier by people who were the ancestors of today's Chemehuevi, but they were not in the same band as Quine's grandfather. He did not know exactly what had been intended centuries earlier, but he had his own associations with cupules here that he believed to have aspects in common with the makers' intentions.

In every place where he had seen cupules in this part of the desert, Quine had noticed there was a natural tank, a place where rain water collected and remained available later. The tanks were in rock depressions, frequently surrounded by boulders and brush, and sometimes not visible from even a few feet away. The cupules, etched on more visible rock faces, seemed to indicate the presence of a tank and possibly fresh water, depending on rainfall. Most animals could smell the water from a distance, but humans needed a visual sign.

He had never talked with his late Chemehuevi grandfather about cupules. There were many things he wished they had discussed in their short time together. Quine was a reflective man, like his grandfather, and he had pondered the cupules. One of his thoughts was that they represented the reflection of stars on the surface of the water, telling the viewer, "Here is where stars will reflect, a place of water." Another of his theories, which didn't necessarily supplant the first theory, was that the cupules might represent mosquito eggs, which are deposited and hatched in fresh water. But his current idea was that they also depicted dragonfly eggs. Those eggs hatch in the same temporary pools as the mosquitoes, and the dragonflies prey on mosquitoes in larval form and then as winged adults.

All three of his theories might be true, as they didn't necessarily exclude each other on a counterfactual basis. Or they all might be false, in that the original intention had been to communicate something entirely different. His concepts were true to his own experience, and his personal associations with the cupules. He wouldn't claim his interpretations to be the definitive meaning, or the original intent of the glyphmakers. But it wasn't a topic that he was likely to discuss with anyone he knew at the moment.

Quine felt disconnected from original intentions in any culture. His ethnic heritage was a mix of Serrano, Chemehuevi, Cahuilla, German, English, Welsh, French, Spanish, and maybe some others. But from the plurality of nations in his bloodstream, there was no single voice that consistently spoke up as the leader.

He liked a lot of things about the Chemehuevi and Serrano peoples, but some that he had met didn't recognize him as one of their own. With his jet-black hair and light coppery skin, some people guessed him to be Mexican, or sometimes Italian. He had been raised by several successive pairs of foster parents, who fed him, clothed him, and sent him to public elementary schools where he had learned to read and received good grades.

Then he was enrolled at the Sherman Institute, a military-style boarding school in Riverside, where Natives were taught agriculture, mechanical skills, and other ways to make a living in the twentieth century American society. Native ways and languages were discouraged, but he had listened and learned, and earned a high school diploma there.

The diploma had surprised some. Quine's manner was deceptively taciturn and unassertive, and sometimes his facial expression might seem to be blank when he was deep in thought, puzzling out some conundrum that didn't even occur to others. He frequently paused to consider a situation or concept from the viewpoint of more than one culture. Silently looking at the sky, he might be internally translating words between cultures, considering the similarities as well as the differences and their implications. Or he might just be looking at the sky and its texture in flux. There were always interesting tangents to explore with his mind, like now, here in the high desert mountains, when he delayed his lunch to look at two dragonflies flying between the vertical leaves of a jojoba bush.

One dragonfly was chasing the other, and they flew higher into the air and then over his head, behind him and out of sight. Then he saw that there was a third dragonfly, motionless on a low leaf, waiting for a mosquito or gnat to present itself. Quine found himself wondering: why did English-speaking people name a real insect after a mythological beast? Dragons and dragonflies had little in common other than wings. Dragonflies didn't breathe fire, and dragons probably didn't eat mosquitoes intentionally. He knew some Native names and nicknames for the dragonfly, and those names could be translated as "pond hawk" and "mosquito hunter." They seemed like good names, descriptive and accurate. But the Spanish word for the insect, *libélula*, was what he preferred to use, partly because of its sound as it rolled off the tongue. It was the diminutive of *libéla*, a Latin-derived word that was not often used in New World Spanish. It referred to a level, as in a level scale, balanced on both sides. The *libélula* was a creature of balance above all, with its two pairs of wings on either side of the fulcrum-like thorax, and its long abdomen acting as counterweight and tail rudder.

Quine had read about the order of insects called *Odonata* in library books at Riverside, but he learned more when his grandfather was still alive, and they watched the *libélulas* together. His grandfather had pointed out that *libélulas* could fly equally well in six directions, the four compass points as well as up and down. East. West. North. South. Earth. Sky. And when a dragonfly hovered in mid-air, balanced and centered, it exemplified the seventh direction, the center, the soul of it all.

He paused for a moment, closed his eyes, and let his awareness hover at its center.

6

All Astir

Seated on the flat near the Anaconda shaft, Stan waited for the others to return from lunch. One leg was extended to the front of him, stretching the hamstrings. Three black-throated sparrows were rummaging beneath a creosote a few feet away. He noticed Jem making his way down the steep part of the wash, sometimes turning his body sideways and stepping with the front foot perpendicular while reaching an elbow back for balance.

Then his eye was caught by the zygodactyl steps of a roadrunner, moving parallel to Jem's descent, but about twenty yards ahead of him on more level ground. As Stan noticed the roadrunner, it hunched low and intently accelerated towards the wash, then lunged and tried to grab something but missed, tapping the sand with open beak. Then it lifted its head and refocused on other nearby prey. Stan saw that the roadrunner had been moving ahead of Jem in stealth, watching for birds or lizards that he startled downhill, and ready to pounce. Jem was the roadrunner's collaborator, but with his eyes looking down at the rocky slope, he was unaware of his role.

A few yards uphill from the shaft entrance, there was another small plateau with scattered creosote, yellow-blooming wildflowers, and grass that was mostly brown and dormant except for one patch of green. It was a popular area for birds and wildlife. Now three Gambel's quail couples were grazing, along with a few sparrows and mourning doves. A couple of the ever-watchful doves were the first to see the roadrunner as it accelerated beak-first into the group, and as the doves flew, they produced a whistle that oscillated between pitches, which was heard for only a split second before the birds were all astir with a startled ripple of flapping sounds and vocalized alarm.

When he first arrived in the desert, Stan had noticed that the doves' alarm whistle was in time with their beating wings. But more recently he realized that the whistled beats were actually the sound of the wings themselves, forcefully moving air. The sound stopped as soon as each dove held its wings out to glide, or landed with its wings folding. He could still hear the dove wings whistle as the roadrunner lunged for the nearest sparrow and missed, thwarted by its practiced evasion. Then the roadrunner lowered its crest and hopped onto a creosote branch to perch, hoping to ambush the first returning bird.

Stan sat cross-legged in the sand, feeling the sun on his face and arms, enjoying the moderate temperature. A light, localized rain earlier in the month had greened the grass at this spot on the hillside, and the creosotes opened their small yellow blossoms afterwards. It'll be a shame to have to go down in that mine when it's so nice up here, he thought. In the stillness before the birds returned to the clearing, he heard the click of a pebble dislodged by Jem's descent. After the pebble bounced to a stop, the silence resumed, the daytime desert in its natural state. It was a silence he had never known in

Chicago, where there was always some noise coming from somewhere and the eardrum was a moving membrane that never rested.

The desert silence amazed him still, and it was a new reality to inhabit, where the external and internal quiet allowed everything else to bloom and burst against its backdrop. He was starting to like it most of the time, but when he first arrived, halted by two flat tires outside of Twentynine Palms, the silence had seemed eerie and foreboding. Sometimes he was nostalgic for the background clatter and low-level buzz of city life, which once seemed normal to him, like the murmur of friendly conversation in an adjoining room.

Almost every day at this time, the miners would move from the calm of the open desert down into the loudness of the mine, with dynamite exploding, clanging picks, hammers striking monzogranite, and shovels scraping. It was extreme even when wearing earmuffs. He welcomed the silence at the surface as an antidote.

A couple inches of water remained in the shaded tank near the cupules. Quine scooped some of it with the small canteen, noticing the water looked and smelled a couple days old. He would take this water to a concave rock near the mine, where the birds would appreciate it. The water in his main canteen was fresh from the well at Twentynine Palms. He took a couple sips, then ate a mesquite cake from his bag. A *libélula* still circled around the area, and Quine figured that it had recently hatched and metamorphosed at this tank, or in a couple of *morteros* nearby. He sat on a flat-topped rock for a moment, feeling the air and seeing the sky.

Then he stood up and began walking back to the mine. His

two canteens brushed together as he walked, and it made him think of a Chemehuevi song that he had heard as a young boy. It was a song to sing while walking, something about drinking gourds clicking together. It had been many years since he had heard the song, and he could only remember a few words and their marching cadence. But he sang those words softly to himself as he walked, and the clacking of the canteens formed a rhythm with the song and his stride.

7

The Try-Works

The weathered lumber of the head frame groaned as William and Stan turned the crank of the windlass. With every revolution of the crankshaft, another length of chain wrapped around the horizontal barrel at the top of the frame, and the load was lifted closer to the surface. They strained at the upward pull, and pushed into the downward thrust with arms extending.

On the first days, the Captain had synchronized their movements with verbal commands as if they were oarsmen, but soon they internalized the rhythm. Yet Haberman continued with his instructions in circular repetition, peppered with spontaneous commentary and playful jibes.

Jem and the Captain stood on opposing sides of the head frame, leaning against the posts to stabilize. It held strong on the vertical axis but was rickety from east to west. "If we keep bringing up decent payloads, I'll invest in a friction hoist. It uses a counterweight, and can handle larger loads. Or maybe a capstan, like we used to spool rope on ship."

Jem and William nodded as they kept working, and Stan

smiled a little. He had noticed that every phase of the mining operation existed in two forms to the Captain: its current incarnation in the physical world, with limitations and malfunctions; and the ideal form that he envisioned, with modernized equipment and streamlined methodologies.

"How about one of those portable gas engines with a pulley to hoist the load?" asked Jem. "It wouldn't take three or four of us to run it."

"Well, sure, that's a possibility too," said Captain Haberman. "One more crank . . . easy now, like the stork delivering a babe," counseled Haberman as the load emerged at the top of the shaft. Almost three hundred pounds of ore were being hoisted in a packet of dusty canvas, lifted by chains hooked to corner grommets. "Brake it," he barked as both Stan and William were already reaching for the brake and lock.

When the load stabilized, Stan reached up with a hooked pole and unlatched the swing arm. Then he hooked the large eyelet at the end of the steel-reinforced arm, and pulled to pivot the arm ninety degrees. The other three reached under the load to guide and stabilize the weight as it swung over the truck bed. When the bundle of ore was directly over the truck, Stan disengaged the brake lock, and the others guided the load into place. "That's it," said Haberman. "The total load's probably a ton and a quarter, all I want to handle with this truck. Then you add me and Jem, that's another ton," he joked.

William leapt onto the rim of the truck bed, grabbed one of the stakes with his left hand, and used his right hand to reach in and unhook the chains from each corner of the canvas. The chains swung inward and the hooks clinked together, then dangled and swayed as the four corners of the canvas fell to the truckbed. Then he jumped off, and they pulled the canvas to reposition it over the ore. Stan said, "Load in, unchocking now" toward the cab, where the Captain and Jem had seated themselves. William and Stan pulled out the wheel chocks, and the Ford started with a roar and then settled into a purr. After a couple weeks of repetitions, the process of hoisting and loading ore had become a smooth teamwork.

"You fellas keep on chipping and blasting. Jem will probably be staying overnight at the mill, and I'll be back in a couple hours."

William nodded, and Stan said, "All right, Captain, hope it's a moneymaker."

Haberman engaged the clutch and shifted into low, and the truck slowly descended the two-rut ramp down the hillside to the open desert. He and Jem both glanced at the stone corral area where Jem's truck was parked as they weaved around three boulders that were shaped like potatoes. Soon they were southbound on the good road, headed to the mill.

"This a '28?" asked Jem.

"1929 AA, one of Henry's best," replied the Captain.

"Much better than the T."

"You know it. This four-speed has torque, really digs in." The road curved through the monzogranite boulder groupings and hills that lined the valley. They gradually ascended to an area where more Joshua trees reached, and the Captain slowed to cross over a dry wash.

"That wash used to be a shortcut to a few places, 'til there was a landslide that blocked the canyon." The Captain slowed for a rocky patch, ore clattering in the truck bed, and weaved a flat path through the jagged bedrock. "After a rain sometimes it's like a river across the road here. Impassable." The Captain gestured from right to left to indicate the flow. "That wash doesn't look like much. But it carries a lot of rainfall off the mountain, and other washes and side canyons connect with it."

"We had some flooding in the hill country back in Texas, but it wasn't like it gets here. These mountains are more steep and rocky, they don't absorb rain," said Jem.

"Don't cross moving water unless you can tell exactly how deep it is," advised Haberman as he slowed and swerved around a chunk of rock.

"Ever bust a spring on one of these trucks?" asked Jem.

"No, but I try to take it easy, on account of the tires," replied Haberman. "They've all been patched a time or two, and we're carrying a heavy load. You know, Keane has a truck with steel tires. You feel every bump, but there's never a flat." The truck sagged and squeaked with the weight of the ore.

"I've heard some gossip about this Keane fellow."

"Most of what you heard is probably true. He's been out here a while, had to defend himself a time or two."

"I heard it's a good idea to have a witness when you do business with him."

Haberman made a scornful expression that twisted the corner of his mouth. "Some people like to talk. Gossip and exaggerate. I've done business with him many times, on the up-and-up."

"Well, I trust your opinion, Captain," said Jem.

"Keane has some witnesses that have made him a better man. A couple sons, a daughter, and his wife. His son Wally watches everything he does, and they're raising that family the right way."

"I didn't know he had a family. Must be hard to raise kids

out here."

"There aren't many full-time miners who even try. But Keane does more than mine ore. He buys and sells equipment, does a little ranching, and still owns a mine and some claims. Sometimes both of these stamps here are crushing ore twenty-four hours a day, with a couple trucks in line. Keane charges five dollars a ton to mill the ore, sometimes gives volume discounts. We'll be getting there at a good time, late afternoon."

"More business at the end of the day?"

"Most people roll in closer to sundown, or a little after. I try not to do that, and not just because it's busy."

"Why not?" Jem's words, heard aloud, sounded more challenging than he intended. He started to say something more polite, but then Haberman smiled and spoke.

"I'll tell you why not. In the last hour of daylight, the whole family might be working in the garden, in the shade of the mesquite trees. One time I saw them there from a distance, and I turned around and left before they saw me. In the nicest hour of the day, they were all there, patiently weeding or planting, I couldn't tell which. But they looked happy. I didn't want to interrupt their garden time."

They were silent for a moment as the road went past a landmark boulder, which looked like a giant skull had tumbled downhill and then halted in a state of semi-awareness.

Jem asked, "They keep a garden out here?"

"You bet. Carrots, peas, squash, you name it."

"Is it near the well?"

"Near enough. They have a couple tanks that hold well water, and they run pipes downhill to the garden."

"How do they keep out rabbits, squirrels, and birds?"

"Well, the varmints are most active in the dawn and twilight hours, when people are usually there to guard the crops. They also have chicken-wire fences with steel plates that go underground a couple feet. A few more tricks too. They know when to sprinkle cayenne at the perimeters."

Nonplussed, Jem shook his head. "I come from a long line of farmers, but I didn't know you could grow vegetables in the desert."

"Keane never stops working, all day long. He's smart too. Maybe you can talk to him about gardening if he's around."

"I hope so," Jem replied. "Wouldn't it be good to have some lettuce and peppers growing by the tent cabin?"

Haberman smiled. "Sure. I hope you have a green thumb, young man."

"Now, Captain," said Jem with a smile, "You can call me 'young man,' but I know you're not that old."

"My legs tell me different," replied Haberman with a wry smile. "Now, if you talk to Mr. Ryland Keane, like most people in the desert, you don't necessarily want to ask about their life back east. Let them talk about it if they desire, and Ry probably won't."

"Lots of people make new starts out here. I heard that Mr. Keane had a different name back east."

"Where'd you hear that?"

"In town. I won't mention it."

"Well, not too many people know that. I don't know what happened way back when, but the Ryland Keane you'll meet today is a good man."

"I look forward to meeting him, Captain. Thanks for bringing me along."

"The other guys will get their turn too. If we have to wait in line while they mill other loads, you can stay overnight with the ore. I'll be back around sunrise to pick you up."

"Sounds good."

"The bunkhouse here is clean. Keane doesn't allow drinking or bootlegging, nothing like that."

"Revenuers would hear about it and shut 'em down like those camps in Dale?" asked Jem.

"Well, maybe. A lot of us who have lasted for a few years in the desert have just plain outgrown liquor. If you drink hard, you usually can't work hard enough to make it here, and a bottle costs money. The bootleggers who make good stuff don't have to work the camps, they stay near town and people come to them."

Jem could see how it might appear that way to the Captain, but his own perspective was different. He had been offered enough bootleg liquor to make him think that distilling was one of the area's leading industries. But he had turned it down, for the most part. "I was never all that crazy about hooch either. I like to live in the real world, not the drunk world," said Jem.

"I'll toast to that!" cackled Haberman, lifting his canteen and steering one-handed. "I looked you guys over when I hired you, and I could tell you weren't heavy drinkers. And you and I are the only ones who smoke, but we're careful about it. Too many fires out here."

"Heck, we're in a desert," said Jem.

"You say 'heck?' Sometimes it's hotter than heck," Haberman joked seriously. "Some people can't live here in the summer. You'll see."

"The weather's swell right now, but it still doesn't seem like a good place for fires, outside of a fireplace or fire ring."

"Too many people like fires," declared Haberman. "The desert's too dry for that, most of the time. And windy.

Tinderbox!" They turned onto the spur that led to the mill, with the road weaving between Joshua trees and through boulder groupings. Jem's eyes were drawn to the red barrel cacti that dotted the valley, and then he looked at the rocky slopes of Queen Mountain and its peaks. He saw nolina stems illuminated in the low angle of the late-day sun, months between flowerings, but with a structural beauty like a honeycomb or spider's web. There were occasional calls of phainopepla, wrens, and sparrows from the trees and bushes, sometimes clear enough to hear above the truck's motor and the cargo's rumble. A pair of ravens wheeled overhead, cawing and croaking like frogs.

"I can see why Mr. Keane chose this valley," said Jem. Haberman grunted affirmatively. After a few miles, they reached a wash that divided this part of Queen Valley from an area of dramatic rock formations to the west. Jem had glimpsed the area while driving on Quail Springs Road, where some of the rocks looked like unfinished or accidental sculptures. Some resembled molten lead poured or spilled, and others might take the shapes of animals, or suggest humanoid features. A couple of the rock formations looked like ships, and a few resembled sea creatures floating, submerging, breaching, spouting, or bottom-feeding. Others took the shapes of spheres, blocks, pyramids, or domes, in full dimension as well as halves, fractions, and fragments.

Imaginative people could discern many things. Jem thought to himself, someday I'll get married and have a couple kids, or maybe a few, and I'll bring the family to this place, and let the kids climb all over the rocks while my wife and I watch them and smile.

"Is this your first time at an ore mill?"

Jem thought for a second. "Guess so. Been to grain mills, lumber mills, cotton mills, gin mills."

The Captain chuckled. "I'll tell you what's what as we go along."

They came to a flat, sandy area in front of the mill. There were two other truckloads of ore near the base of the scales and conveyor. The Captain made a three-point turn, backed up to a spot next in line, put the truck in park, and turned off the engine. As they stepped out from the cab, they heard a loud hello from the other side of the hill where the mill had been installed on a concrete slab. Jem saw two men standing, and another seated. The Captain waved and called, "Evening!" with a smile, even though it wasn't quite evening. Their voices were clearly audible because the mill wasn't running at the moment, but they spoke loudly around the machinery as a habit. Jem chocked the truck's wheels with four chunks of ore.

Two of the men picked up long-handled sticks with rubber blades on the end. "Ah, the squeegees," said the Captain to Jem. "They're scraping the gold and mercury off the amalgamation tables into the try-pots. Let's unload the truck here."

The Captain and Jem grabbed shovels, and started unloading ore near the base of the conveyer. It would have to be loaded again to the ore carts when they were available.

"Notice that he has three or four different ore carts," remarked Haberman. Jem looked at the carts with ore from other mines, and saw that one had some worn green paint, one had larger wheels, and one was smaller but sturdy-looking. "They came from different mines, but they all fit this track."

As Haberman and Jem shoveled the ore from the truck to a flat spot, they watched the other miners fill the first ore cart, then push it down the flat part of the track to the weigh station at the beginning of the conveyor incline. As the others turned, they nodded hello to the Captain and Jem, then righted another ore car and rolled it up to the track. Then they lifted and mounted it on the rails for loading. After the last of their ore was transferred, three cars sat heavily on the rails, which would soon use the gasoline-powered winch to convey the first car up the ramp, where it would dump the ore through the grizzly into the hopper to be crushed by the stamps, and then processed with mercury to separate the gold.

"Is one of those men Ryland Keane?" asked Jem.

"No, but the one in the chewed-up hat is his brother-in-law, Lloyd. He usually runs the mill at night. The little guy with the white beard is called Swedish Johnny, because there are a few other Johnnies around. He tried to homestead, but they didn't allow it because he's not a citizen. He still has a couple claims around here."

The Captain glanced up the road to see if any more milling customers were on the way. It was clear. "The older fellow in the rocking chair is Bob Correy. He's been around the desert forever, and lives in a building they built here on Keane's property. His brother was an outlaw, but Bob's a good egg. Let's go over there."

They walked around to the other side of the mill. Swedish Johnny pointed at their truck, and said, "God made man, but Henry Ford put wheels under him."

Captain Haberman chuckled. "That's a good one, Johnny. It's a good one every time."

"Who's the new man?" asked Lloyd, with a smile.

"This is Jem Parker from Texas. He's new to mining, but he's got a good head on his shoulders, and a strong back."

Bob Correy spoke up. "Hello, Jem! Everybody starts some

time. I been mining since last century, still not rich."

Lloyd put down the squeegee. "Glad to meet you. I'm Lloyd. Plenty of new people lately, good for business."

Jem replied with a smile and a wave of the hand. "Good to meet y'all."

The Captain asked, "Lloyd, is Ry going to be around tomorrow morning?"

"He'll be here a little after sunrise, unless something comes up."

"You think he has any clean straight rails, never bent or mangled?"

"Reckon so. He's got the key to that building. I need to paint so you guys can mill." Lloyd crouched down and unlocked a metal box under the amalgamation plate. He took out a brown glass bottle of mercury and a wide-bristled brush. He poured a horizontal line across the top of the sloped copper plate, then used the brush to spread it evenly. Then he poured another line of mercury a few inches lower, and spread it with the brush. Then another line. The thin layer of quicksilver on copper was shaded from direct sun, yet it still gleamed in the shade. Lloyd said, "There's some newpapers over there. Only a few days old."

Bob Correy said, "They have a story you won't like, Joe. Turns out Hoover vetoed the pension increase."

Haberman replied, "What? It went all the way through Congress. Hoover had to get his hands on it."

"You'd figure he'd want to help us soldiers and sailors out," replied Correy. "We've done more for this country than the bankers have."

"You got that right," replied Haberman. "And we thought Hoover would be a friend to miners too, since he used to be one. Nope."

"How many years has an ounce of gold been at $20.64?" asked Jem.

"Too damn many," replied Haberman.

"Dang gold prices, rising everywhere in the world but here. Hoover keeps his thumb on the scale, he's no friend to miners," said Correy.

"How much mining did he ever do, really?" asked the Captain. "He went to school and they called him a mining engineer. He wrote a book on it."

"Probably never got his hands dirty after he graduated," replied Correy.

Haberman walked over to the table. He lifted up the rock that was holding down the papers, then grabbed a small stack. "Sports page here, Jem."

"Salesman from L.A. drove out here, left a fresh paper this morning. Take a look at Roosevelt's radio speech," said Correy. "Right here." He reached for one near the middle of the stack. "Roosevelt from New York state, Teddy's cousin. Listen to what he says. Right on the front page." He found the paragraph, and started reading, "'. . . We need to build from the bottom up and not the top down, put our faith once more in the forgotten man at the bottom of the economic pyramid.' How 'bout that, Joe?"

"Dunno," said Haberman. "I don't trust Democrats and I don't trust Republicans. None of 'em."

"Well, we have to trust somebody to get us out of this mess. This Roosevelt has good ideas." replied Correy.

Swedish Johnny interjected, "Hoover sunk the ship." He looked at the Captain pointedly. "People that used to work for a living, they are broke you know? Have to dig the metal out of the ground." He gestured towards Jem and the Captain.

Haberman spat on the ground. "You're not even a citizen, Johnny. You can't vote."

Johnny shook his fist. "I put my sweat into this country and pay tax everywhere I go. I have my say."

"What navy did you sail for, Johnny? That's one thing you don't talk about."

"More than one. I been around this world, seen plenty of tings."

"Sure, Johnny, you want American gold, but you can't have American soil, you can't homestead, and you can't vote," replied the Captain. "You're not trusted."

Johnny lunged toward Haberman, but Jem stepped between them. Lloyd had put down the brush and mercury jar, and he grabbed Johnny's shoulder from behind. The Captain stood his ground and looked at Johnny contemptuously. After an uncomfortable moment, he stepped away and said, "I have to go. Make sure nobody gives Jem any liquor, he's not even twenty-one."

Lloyd replied, "Joe, you know that doesn't happen here."

The Captain spoke to Jem. "They'll be milling this ore most of the night, might get interrupted a time or two. Keep an eye on both ends of the mill, but get some sleep in the bunkhouse when you can. I'll be back to pick you up at zero six hundred hours."

"Thanks, Captain. See you then." replied Jem, surprised by the Captain's attitude towards Swedish Johnny. "I need to grab my bedroll out of the truck." They walked up the hill to the truck, and Jem took his bedroll from the cab.

"I'm bringing two shovels over there, Jem," called Lloyd. "And we'll have some empty carts for you real soon."

As Lloyd was walking around the hill towards Jem with a pair of shovels, the Captain was driving away in the truck, towards the Anaconda and its tent cabin. As he drove across Queen Valley, the rays of the late-day sun beamed across the landscape and through the passenger window, but he looked straight ahead at the road.

8

The Sphinx

After the sun fell below the horizon and the temperature dropped a few degrees, a yucca moth woke and stirred from his sleeping berth within a Joshua flower. He opened his wings and stretched, then crawled up a petal towards the darkening sky. With only a few days to live, his imperative was to mate with a female moth so that she could produce viable eggs while she pollinated the yuccas and Joshua trees. He did not need to hunt food or seek water during this brief phase of his life; all he needed to do was mate, once, and then more than once if possible.

He had liaisoned successfully and enjoyably with a female moth during the previous evening, and spent the day sleeping deep within the flower. As he climbed, he was already sensing female pheromones nearby, and was eager to mate again. He emerged at the top of a flower petal near the tree's apex, and his silvery-white wings were faintly illuminated by the last rays of the setting sun and a couple bright stars emerging in the east. He was also noticed by the sonar of a nearby bat, and the bat swooped down, grabbed him with his long, sticky tongue, and ate him.

Then the bat darted upwards and immediately began to use echo sounding to locate more insects. He rapidly clicked his vocal cords together to produce a pitch that humans would consider ultrasonic, and he used his throat and mouth as a megaphone to bounce the hypershrill tones off objects to determine their shape, speed, and sometimes texture. There, to his left, he detected a sphinx moth caterpillar drinking the nectar of a flower that some call Fremont's Pincushion, and he dive-bombed the caterpillar, who became aware of a disturbance in air currents and dropped off the flower to the ground just in time. The bat veered away, avoiding entanglement with wildflowers and cacti, where it would become grounded and vulnerable. He flapped, glided, and swerved into the evening sky, shrilling and echoing, listening with hunger. In the sand below the pincushion, the caterpillar lifted his head slightly to look around, resembling the Sphinx for which his species was named.

Jem had the mill bunkhouse to himself, but it was an uneasy sleep. He woke and changed position several times. Though there was a bushy ridge buffering the sound between the mill and the bunkhouse, the percussion and rumble of the rock-crushing stamps echoed across the valley. He checked on the progress twice during the night, following the starlit path over the ridge and back. After the mill paused for a while, he had fallen into a heavy sleep, bone-restful but without dreams.

The Captain's truck returned while it was still dark outside, its headlights briefly lighting an interior wall of the bunkhouse, but Jem didn't wake until the sun came up a few minutes later, hearing the mill pounding again. But then it stopped. He walked over the ridge to the millside plateau, where the Captain was talking with another man that Jem guessed to be Ryland Keane.

"Is that it? Any ore left in the hopper, or stuck in the crusher?" asked Haberman.

"No, it all went through," replied Keane.

Haberman began to twist his shoulder slightly, then touched his other arm, moved his disabled leg forward then back, a series of fluid movements that looked like he was trying to suppress anger. "What about the plates? Your man been keeping them clean?"

Keane looked at him evenly and replied in a steady voice. "Lloyd told me that he scraped the apron clean before the first load, Joe. And that *your* man was here watching him."

"Blazes!" replied Haberman. "You mean to tell me there was only a quarter-ounce of gold in that whole truckful? We can't make it on that."

Arms folded, Keane looked at Haberman impassively, like some weather-beaten rock figure that had survived the desert's changes. "Joe, I told you before that nobody's made money off the Anaconda for a couple decades now. You were doing okay for a while, but whatever you found is probably played out."

Haberman noticed Jem with his bedroll under his arm. "C'mon Jem, let's get out of here. We'll go back to the mine and dig up some more worthless rock. I'll have to cut your pay if this keeps up." He turned away towards the truck.

Keane had seen dozens of miners come and go over the years, working hard but going broke. Some of them had worse tempers than Haberman. He had known Joe Haberman for a few years, and had a working relationship with him. "Joe, come back when you're ready to sit down and drink a cup of coffee, and I'll meet your junior miners. Some loads are good, some not so good. That's how the game plays out." Haberman kept walking in silence, but waved goodbye in a way that seemed normal.

9

Does the Whale Diminish?

Under a darkening sky, hundreds of Joshua trees cast jagged, distended shadows. It was a half-hour before sunset, and Haberman moved a little slower. After a busy day in the mine, both knees, both hips, and his back were aching. He thought about finding some medicine to nullify the pain, but just as quickly told himself no.

In the last twenty-four hours, he had lost his temper a couple times, and was disappointed in himself. But he was also still irked at those that he felt had provoked his anger. He had parked near the base of the mountain and now walked along its perimeter, looking for the right level place with clean sand, where he intended to sit quietly for a few minutes before going to the cabin. The place he chose this evening was equidistant between two large but dissimilar Joshua trees, flanking him like pillars of eccentricity.

Sitting cross-legged in soft sand, he focused on his breathing. With conscious deliberation, he inhaled slowly through his nose. Then he exhaled through the mouth gently, as his teacher had told him, "like a long whisper to a trusted universe." As

57

he inhaled, he appreciated the freshness of the mountain air. When he let the breath out, he felt tension leaving his body and dissolving into the desert's grounded and charged atmosphere. Only here had he found this kind of calmness, in the silence of the desert, beginning in the eleventh year after the war had ended on the eleventh day of the eleventh month.

The focused breathing was a calming technique he had learned a couple of years into the war, when a shipmate noticed that he was "getting the heebie jeebies," as they said at the time. Ensign Charlie Fall was a few years older than most of the sailors, enlisting before the war. He had traveled the world in more peaceful times, and spoke three languages well. He had a steadiness and thoughtfulness that Haberman and the others respected. Charlie had spent some years in Tokyo and Hokkaido, where he had been invited into temples and local homes for tea ceremonies and meditation. "You might find this practice invaluable," he said to Haberman, and he did, very much at times. But lately his attention had been wavering.

During his first attempts at meditation, back on ship, the focus on breathing had led to moments where he had verged on hyperventilating, and there were times when he briefly held his breath between cycles. This wasn't beneficial. He found that his conscious mind was trying to control the breathing, overthinking the process. Applying the mind to full concentration without control was a skill that involved reframing and stepping back. He learned to observe the natural rhythm of his breathing without interfering. It required a detachment that resembled indifference, while still being deeply involved and present.

The concept, as Charlie had taught him, was simply to sit and breathe, without any particular thoughts in his mind; to be, for some moments, like an empty ship on a calm sea. There might intermittently arise some specific ideas or images, which were to be observed with the same detachment, uninvolved with any emotion or agenda. He might find himself thinking of a place he had lived, or someone he had known, or a task that needed to be done. Each of these thoughts were allowed to pass through the consciousness and then beyond, without fixation.

For Haberman, a breakthrough came when he realized that some aspects of meditation were like looking out a port hole below ship. Various objects, creatures, and scenes might float past the port hole, but they didn't require action or opinion. Some pink coral might appear, then an octopus, then an old boot. Observe them existing in the world without judgement or hierarchy as they come and go, he told himself. Do the same when thoughts cross the mind while meditating.

He could understand the outer world better when it was slightly detached from the inner self, and he could objectively see the points of connection and potential convergence, though he would visualize more than articulate the patterns.

Over time, he also found this practice causing him to look at people and situations more dispassionately, seeing them exist and proceed for their own reasons that had almost nothing to do with him. Their relation to him was not as ally or enemy, not as superior or subordinate. He saw everyone as an equal being, breathing in the same universe as an independent entity.

It made him think more of "We" than "I." He had seen this concern for others to greater and lesser degrees among higher-ranking officers, usually lesser. He wanted to demonstrate, to himself and others, that the "we" mentality, an egalitarian attitude, was still a successful model long after the days of its archetype with Noah and the ark. He had never Captained a ship while in the Navy, though now he was the *de facto* Captain of this mining crew.

His thoughts were drifting again. Breathe in. Breathe out.

Breathe in.

Breathe out.

Breathe in.

Through the port hole of his mind, from where he sat in the high desert, he saw a Joshua tree, its limbs seeming to gesture elsewhere while in the middle of calisthenics. It was as if the species had been frozen akimbo during a historic disaster that only Joshua trees had witnessed and understood.

Breathe out.

Breathe in. Savor the breath and what it brings.

Breathe out.

Breathe in.

He looked at the Joshua tree through a spyglass in his mind, studying the off-green spikes that jutted like pineapple tops. They presented awkwardly to the sky bouquets of blossoms that were the color of cream tinged with sand and sunlight.

Breathe out.

Breathe in.

In his mind he leaned into a Joshua blossom, and its aroma wasn't sweet, exactly; more like a long jar of fireflies with a spoonful of crushed almonds and some mystery ingredient at the bottom of the jar.

Breathe out. BAM. What was that? He started and took a short, sharp breath. BAM! That.

It was that again. It felt like an earth tremor, not uncommon in this desert. But he knew it was something else, the ingrained memory of an incident on a Navy ship in cold November waters, more than eleven years earlier. Now the odor was like almonds mixed with brine and his own cold sweat. BAM. Through the port hole of his mind, he saw something large and light-colored, colliding sidelong with the ship.

German submarines were known to be in the area. But that was not what he saw. What he saw had an eye that was looking in his direction, if not directly at him. He saw a lower jaw full of teeth that were the size and shape of traffic cones in the mouth of the world's largest carnivore: teeth slightly worn from grinding squid, jellyfish, and whatever crossed its path, from plankton to human. What he saw was an air-breathing, warm-blooded mammal like himself, with a nervous system, a brain, and consciousness.

What Haberman did not know at the time, and would never know with certainty, was whether the whale had been trying to harm the ship, which it did not, or whether it had intended to alert them of harm to come, which it did. Immediately after it swam away, a pair of torpedoes raked the ship from bow to stern on the left side, causing it to tip and then capsize. Twenty-four men had died while the survivors were piling into lifeboats or grabbing flotsam. Haberman suffered a broken tibia, impacted kneecap, and torn ligaments in his leg, and he would have lifelong issues with alignment and disks in his back. But his friend who taught him how to meditate, Ensign Charles Fall, was a casualty of the attack, only a few days before the war ended. Charlie would never make it back to the Zen temple.

Haberman shook his head, and looked at the sand. It looked like a desert, but felt like a beach. This was once an ocean, he thought, and it will be so again. The ebb-tide has lasted centuries, well beyond its neap. He raised his gaze to the Joshua trees and the mountains, and appreciated their beauty as if seeing them for the first time. Why was he thinking of the war now? He intended to meditate in peace. Why had the whale followed him here, followed his thoughts, hundreds of miles from the Pacific Ocean to this vast, dry desert?

He stood up slowly, and it took a few seconds for his legs to feel comfortable on land. He started back to camp. As he walked through the desert, he tried not to think of whales. He breathed in, and he breathed out.

10

The Counterpane

J em pulled into Ned's Service Station, east of Four Corners in Twentynine Palms. It was a few minutes before nine p.m., and there were no other customers. Ned walked over with a smile. "'Lo there, Jem! Been a little while."

"Evening, Ned. Good to see you." Jem stepped out of the truck and shook hands with Ned. "I could use a buck's worth of regular."

Ned started pumping the gas while Jem stretched and looked around. Adjacent to the station was Palmhaven Cabins, a travelers' motor court with two rows of adobe *casitas* that were rented by the night, week, or month. At either end of the courtyard between the *casitas* grew a few palm trees, which shaded the center pavilion and its picnic tables. Jem had last sat at one of the pavilion tables about three weeks earlier, when he and Stan, also a Palmhaven lodger at the time, decided to apply for mining jobs after seeing Haberman's "Help Wanted" posting at the American Legion.

"Been busy at the mine?" asked Ned.

"You know it. Six days a week," replied Jem. "We have to

break down a mountain of rock to get a little gold."

"How much gold does anybody find out there these days?"

"We find just enough to get by. Think you could use some help in the garage some time? Holiday weekends coming up?"

"Memorial Day weekend, definitely. Plenty of tourists with car trouble every year."

"How's business otherwise?"

"There's more business than money to pay for it. Travelers and drifters and grifters, passing through. The locals are steady though."

"Well, I can fix tires and tubes, replace fan belts, radiator hoses, crankcase service, repairs, other things too."

"You were a big help last time. The holiday crowd can pay the going rate for those jobs."

"Any rooms available for tonight?" Jem gestured towards the Palmhaven.

"Cabin Eight, fifty cents. Friends and family rate," smiled Ned.

"Sounds good. Think your sisters are still awake?"

"The living room lights went out a few minutes ago. They'll be around tomorrow morning though."

"Okay. Thanks, Ned." Jem paid for the room and gas, then pulled around to park behind Cabin Eight. He was looking forward to a full night's sleep, without the snoring that sometimes rattled the Anaconda cabin.

Back at the Anaconda, Stan was beginning to fall asleep on his cot. He looked up at the wall of the tent cabin, and reached up to touch one of the wall's stones with the palm of his hand. It still felt warm several hours after sunset. Like adobe or masonry, stone could work as a heat sink. All afternoon, the west wall had absorbed sunshine and 75 degree heat. In the evening, as the outdoor temperature dropped to 55°F, the walls radiated a subtle warmth. Stan's red plaid blanket was under his knees near the foot of the cot, unneeded for now, though he might use it after midnight as the cabin cooled. He soon fell into sleep, and snored almost inaudibly.

Near the east wall, Quine was already asleep in a cot, curled on his side with a doubled-over pillow under his head. After a few minutes, he began to dream, and in the dream, he was in a cave that was about the same size as the tent cabin. The cave seemed familiar to him. The walls and floor were monzogranite boulders with a high quartz content, near white in color, illuminated by sunlight that shone through gaps between large boulders that formed the cave's roof. The sunlight, natural skylights, and bright quartz made the cave seem cheerful. Unusual for a cave, but not so strange in a dream. There were gaps in the walls like windows and doorways that led to other cave chambers.

The gigantic boulders that roofed the caves were adjacent to one another like the last few apples in a bowl, and the rocks below had been further hollowed to expand each room. Small alcoves, between boulders, had sandy floors where *ollas* and other personal items could be buried and marked with spirit sticks. There were cool, shaded areas where food could be stored, and an outdoor patio with *morteros* for milling and mixing. Fire pits had rock chimneys, and there were berth areas with soft, level sand for sleeping. Petroglyphs and cupules were near a natural tank. Each cave room had two or more gap portals that connected to the outside, or to other caves. Sometimes a waist-high ledge in one room would become the floor of the next room uphill. In his dream, he saw all these things, and they were familiar.

After examining the boulder roof and its sunlit edges, he was surprised to look down and see that the white quartz cave was full of people, seated closely on ledges and the floor. In this dream, he was at the back of the cave, and the people were looking away from him, towards a small, offset grotto around a corner near the front entrance. They did not seem to be aware of his presence, but he felt in the room a sense of anticipation and joy to a degree he had rarely known in waking life. But he only felt it for a moment, for just as he started to look more closely at the people in the dream, he heard the varied birdcall of a thrasher in the near distance outside the tent cabin. For a moment of transition, the dream world merged with the physical universe, and he heard the thrasher's call echo inside the quartz cavern of his dream. But then he woke fully into the tent cabin, and listened again.

Perched on a pinyon pine, a California Thrasher sang his repertoire of other birds' songs. A moment earlier, he had noticed an animal skulking through the shadows beyond a bramble of catclaw acacia and brittlebushes. With clouded starlight and an obscured crescent moon, he couldn't see exactly what animal was there, but it moved like a predator, maybe an uncommon one like a badger or ring-tailed cat. The thrasher had flown straight to the pine from the hidden place where his mate guarded four turquoise eggs.

By singing various bird songs a short distance from the nest, he hoped to distract and deflect the predator to hunt elsewhere. At least one of his repeated calls, the 'kree-kree' of a prairie falcon, might intimidate a badger or ring-tailed cat, but wouldn't fool a fox or bobcat. After a few seconds of his singing, he listened and looked, and sensed the low dark shadow of the predator slink away through the bushes and beyond the ridge. He flew back to the nest, which was comfortably lined with grass, fuzzy creosote seedballs, and a strip of faded cloth. Folding and relaxing his wings at each side, and then legs beneath him, he eased into the nest with his mate and their eggs, and soon they were silently asleep.

11

The Lee Shore

Eight shades of paint between beige and brown were arrayed in dabs, and she was mixing a ninth with her palette blade. Another specific beige was needed to depict some facets of the craggy block of stone in the foreground. In every season but summer, Lee favored the mid-afternoon for painting. The light during those hours seemed to change more slowly than at sundown or in the early morning. She was not a fast painter, and usually spent more time looking and seeing than applying brush strokes. She needed to see a landscape clearly and in detail to paint it, and she needed the seeing more than the painting. But the discipline of painting was how she focused and saw the desert most clearly.

In her job at the motor court, she met some who came to the desert for gold, some who thought they could find oil, some associated with aqueducts, pipelines, or railroads. Some for land to buy or sell. There were those who came for artifacts, and a few seeking turquoise or silver. Others came for quartz and unusual rocks. Some of her least favorite visitors came to dig up cacti and other desert plants. But many who came to the desert didn't necessarily want to possess any part of it; they wanted to experience and understand it. There were also some who were trying to get away from something, and others who came to seek what they needed, in the desert or within themselves. If you talked a person long enough, or sometimes not very long at all, you found that many came to both escape and seek, to elude one thing and find another, though sometimes they turned out to be the same.

Lee was drawn to the desert and its creatures, colors, and moods, its mix of jagged lines and graceful contours, and she felt that seeing and painting would be her path into knowledge. After a few years, she loved the desert even more, and didn't like to leave it, even temporarily. With her lightly freckled skin shaded by a wide-brimmed hat, she sat and looked at everything, motionless except for respiration and eye movement. Then she would pause her breath before exhaling, and the sweep of her gaze would focus on various objects and locations. Pause and focus would frequently happen in the same instant, so that respiration and vision were two synchronized components in a state of mind similar to meditation, but also linked in a larger process of seeing and being.

She looked at the block of gneiss, then looked again, and kept looking. It was cloven like the inverted hoof of a bighorn sheep. A large fissure bisected it, and each half was gnarled and cracked like petrified wood. The block gathered darkness when a cloud passed overhead, then it was sunlit again, and it hulked over a red barrel cactus that presented two golden buds as briefly available offerings to pollinators. She figured that the blooms would be painted last, and might be the easiest subjects in the painting. She looked again at the stone with its juts and crags that had endured for millennia, illuminated with the changing light of the season and moment. She kept looking.

Shaking the cart over the truck bed, Stan watched the smaller rocks rattle into place around and atop the other monzogranite. Some of the chunks had a certain cast in the sunlight, a dusky shine, that he hadn't seen at the Anaconda. Stan had agreed to work a few hours on this bright Saturday morning. "There are things that need muscle and brains, but mostly muscle, and your height helps too," the Captain had told him. In exchange for a half-day's work, he would receive a full day's pay. They were at one of Haberman's claims on a rocky slope near the Pinto Mountain range. The truck could make it far enough up the canyon, but it couldn't negotiate the narrow, jagged side-wash that was its tributary. The smaller wash, draining into the larger, reminded Stan of a side street in the city, which could feed into a major street more than twice as wide, with more traffic and larger buildings.

There might be any number of canyons and washes radiating downward from the top of a mountain. He thought of the roads in Chicago that radiated out from the downtown lakefront like fingers on a hand, reaching through the city blocks for miles into the countryside. Then his thoughts turned like an automobile to a quiet side street lined with trees and homes, two-flats, and apartment buildings. On each residential side street in a neighborhood, thought Stan, there might be people that you should know, or maybe someday would meet. Maybe even someone who would play a major role in your life, a friend or collaborator or lover perhaps, sitting in a chair near a window, maybe listening to a radio or reading a book, unknown to you now, and likewise you to them. There might be a person for whom you were ideally suited in some ways, but your paths would never cross. Or maybe they would? In the city, there was a chance. But there were so few people to meet here in the high desert, remote, unsettled, and extreme.

There were only a couple hundred people living in the entire Morongo Basin, according to the census, which probably missed a few. But there were hundreds more when the weekenders came "sniping" for gold. They drove here from the cities, through the mountain passes with their flivvers and jalopies rattling with tools and kettles, and pans that could be used to fry breakfast and then maybe find gold.

In most of human history, people had come from the rural areas to the towns or cities to make their fortunes. But with bank failures and mass unemployment in the cities, people were commuting to the mountains and deserts to find what gold remained. With cars and trucks that had rolled off the assembly lines sparkling and affordable in better times, they covered ground quicker than the horses, mules, and wagons of the last gold rush. Sometimes the weekend miners were families or young couples, looking for gold, hiking, and maybe having a picnic. But mostly they were determined individuals who had been smacked around by the crash and panic, yet still believed that some combination of luck and effort would produce nuggets of wealth, or at least enough gold dust to buy a couple meals.

Although he had been making a living at it for only three weeks, Stan considered himself a mining professional, one of a couple dozen in the area. But the existence for most miners was hand to mouth. He grabbed the flat shovel and used it to prod the ore more evenly across the truck bed. Room for a couple more cartloads, he thought. Then he caught a movement on the mountain in his peripheral vision, and glanced up at the boulder formation for a moment. Stillness.

His thoughts returned to the roads in Chicago, which had been designed and built by more than one culture, over centuries, using dissimilar concepts for similar purposes. Yet the systems co-existed and co-informed one another. It was pleasant for him now to think of these distant roadways and envision their geometry, as on a chalkboard or map. The streets that radiated in diagonals to and from downtown were built on Native trails that aligned with natural features like ridges and waterways. Most angled towards the mouth of the Chicago River at Lake Michigan. As European-Americans later traversed and transgressed, these trails were paved and given names like Clark, Ridge, Lincoln, Milwaukee, Elston, Grand, Archer, Ogden, and Vincennes. These converging/radiating trails along natural topologies were the Native American concept.

The European-American schematic for Chicago streets, overlaid and complementing the Native system, represented a grid pattern drawn eight blocks to the mile. Streets were categorized East or West, North or South, depending on their directional radius from the downtown intersection of State and Madison. This central spot would be (0,0) if the streets were seen as axes in a graph. A block was regarded as a unit of distance equaling one-eighth of a mile, and there was usually a corner at the end of each block, but not always. The buildings in the first block were assigned addresses from 1 to 99, N., S., E., or W., even-numbered on the north and west side of the street, odd-numbered on the south and east. The 800 block, in each direction, would be exactly one mile away, the

1600 block would be two miles away, and so on, with some arcane exceptions known to the savvy. These multiples of 800 were the major streets, usually two lanes in each direction, with stop signs at minor intersections and stoplights at major, and clusters of shops and offices between homes, apartments, garages, and churches, near schools and factories. It all made sense to him. Sometimes he missed Chicago.

Stan rolled the empty cart up the hill, sometimes lifting it over rocks and ridges, still ruminating on the rays and grids of the Chicago street system. Its known and measured qualities appealed to him now, here in this near-wild place that had not been completely explored or understood, though it had been surveyed and baselined almost a hundred years earlier by Colonel Henry Washington, George's nephew. The two-dimensional grid is pure Cartesian geometry, Stan thought. The Chicago street system, as well as the desert's baselines, would be understandable to Euclid, who wrote about lines and planes in the third century B.C. But the civic engineers of the modern era used this geometry for practical uses. Given any two addresses on the Chicago street grid, a person could calculate the distance between those two points, as well the compass direction of travel.

Now his mind flashed back to a night in Chicago in the last weeks of winter, with sooty snow on the curbs and parkways, not long before he left the city. He had been driving a taxi part-time during his junior year of college. After dropping off a fare at a brick two-flat near the intersection of Kedzie and Diversey, he was flagged down by a middle-aged man in a gabardine coat and Homburg hat. "You know where Little Ben's is at?"

"Yes, sir," replied Stan. He had taken other fares to the

speakeasy. "Up on Montrose."

The man affirmed, "That's it."

Just west of Cicero, thought Stan. On the linear streets of the grid, he could take Kedzie from Diversey (2800 W.) up to Montrose (4400 W.). Subtracting 28 from 44 is sixteen blocks, which is two miles. The westward leg of the journey, turning left on Montrose, would be eighteen blocks, another two miles plus. So it would be a little over four miles on the grid route.

Yet there was a quicker way. The Milwaukee Avenue diagonal radiated northwest through the intersection of Cicero and Montrose. He turned onto Milwaukee while envisioning it as the hypotenuse of a right triangle, the realm of the Pythagorean Theorem. In a practiced, split-second calculation, he sized each two-mile leg of the triangle and squared them. Then he added them together to yield eight. The length of the Milwaukee hypotenuse would be the square root of that number, a little less than three miles.

So the diagonal route would be more than a mile shorter than the right angle of the grid, and more direct. He marveled again on the range of cultures that informed this quick calculation: Ojibwe, Potawatomie, Miami, English, French, Greek, Arabic, and American. The two dimensions of the line and three dimensions of the plane could be expanded to the fourth dimension, going back into history with various minds observing the physical world over time. But what about the future?

"So you're the Stanicek kid." The passenger was looking at Stan's cab license, mounted on the dashboard. They were at a four-way stop, and Stan glanced back at him in the rearview mirror, his thoughts interrupted.

"Yes," replied Stan flatly. "Are you from my neighborhood?"

The man grunted, or maybe that was how he laughed. "Well, let's just say I know your family. I saw your father at a little shindig last night, and let's just say I hope you drove him home. Or maybe another hack did." He chuckled another abrasive monosyllable that sounded like someone dropping a sanding block on a hardwood floor.

Stan said nothing for a moment. He had been almost asleep at two a.m. when he heard his father slam the door and stumble, cursing in more than one language. But he knew the old man had driven himself home, irresponsible yet lucky, his regular combination. Stan looked again into the rearview mirror at the passenger, then focused on the street ahead. "My father made it home okay. May I ask your name, sir?"

"Oh, you don't have to worry about my name. It's better if you don't know it. Let's just say that I have some connections with the group that funded your scholarship. I get reports about you, they say you're a smart fellow and you're gonna stay that way."

Stan was puzzled. As far as he knew, his scholarship was funded by a local civic group comprised of well-known alumni and businessmen. This guy seemed shady. Stan came to a stop sign, stepped on the brake, looked both ways, and glanced back in the mirror for a split-second. Then he drove on.

The passenger took a sip from a flask and continued, "When you get your degree, you should try to work for the city, or one of the big engineering outfits. You can help us there."

Stan still said nothing. He thought for a second that he had been confused for someone else, but the man knew Stan's name and his interest in engineering. Apparently he also knew his father.

The passenger continued. "You know what, bud? It's a two-way street we got here, not just this street but our path in life. Somebody does something for you, you do something for them. There may come a day when we ask something of you. Or maybe that day will never come. But be ready. Don't be looking at the world through a beer glass like your old man. Pull over here."

He pulled to the curb, still trying to understand what had been said to him, by who, and why. The man tossed a five-dollar bill onto the seat, several times the price of the fare. "Keep your mouth shut and your nose clean, Stanny boy. Chicago is still a moneymaking town." He barked his laugh, then opened the door and stepped onto the curb, slammed the door and walked away.

Stan sat parked on Montrose for a moment, trying to process the man's comments. Was some kind of criminal syndicate financing his education? Was he bound to them, beholden to their agenda, whatever it was? Then he noticed a few people huddled in the doorway of a shuttered wig store next to the speakeasy. One of them stumbled up to the cab. "Got a nickel, a dime, mister?" Stan looked him in the eye. He was about the same age as Stan, but weather-beaten and unshaven, wearing filthy clothes. Stan gave him the five-dollar bill from the fare, and drove away, still distracted.

A couple weeks after that incident, his father crashed his sedan through the display window of a department store, and then assaulted the store manager and a police officer. He was sentenced to two years in jail. Not long after that, Stan received a letter that discontinued his scholarship. After he finished the semester's classes with good grades, he withdrew from school, packed up his Studebaker, and headed west.

Different places, different faces. Always new things to learn, he thought. There was great uncertainty about the future, but that was true for everyone. He shoveled ore into the cart, whistling along with the birds, enjoying the desert sunshine and the warmth of spring. He was glad to be here now.

Nose up. Jaws shut. Nary a howl nor yip. Sensing the wind, concealed by a yucca. Scurry to the cover of a rock, past a scrub pine. Then a low-bellied trot through the canopy of a flowering creosote, and a quick slink to boulders with a better view. The coyote was looking to observe more than hunt. It was odd to see a human, and then two more humans, here on this side of the mountain. Watching from above, the coyote had seen a young woman, sitting with a stick in her hand, looking across the valley. Now, after several leaps and strolls across two dry washes, he was looking at a man in a cap, wearing gloves, hitting a rock with a large tool that clanged. Another man, taller and younger, was clanking a cart down a slope towards a truck, stopping to lift the cart's wheels over a rock.

The coyote had been whelped wary of the human species, and people had shot at him in the past. He studied the way they moved, and took interest in how their hands used tools. To the coyote, humans seemed skilled, peculiar, and dangerous.

Most animals are either nocturnal or diurnal, and some who favor the twilight are called crepuscular, like the deer. But the coyote roams and hunts day or night, using surprise and guile. Hunting in packs at night, mostly solo during the day, they try to vary their patterns. What other creature can be seen unpredictably at any hour of the day or night, and in almost any location? Humans, akin to the coyote in this way and others. The coyote knew.

Haberman took a couple steps back from the overhang and placed his pick on top of a flat rock. After being hunched over the claim for most of an hour, he needed to stretch his back and shoulders. He reached his arms into the air and flexed his fingers, then noticed a bighorn sheep on top of the ridge, forty yards away and curious.

He knew at first glance that it was a ewe, distinguishable from the ram by her thinner face and smaller horns, as well as her less powerful shoulders and haunches. Her left horn was mostly gone, leaving a stub that was smaller than her ear. How would that happen? A male bighorn might lose parts of his spirals by ramming against other males to assert dominance, or to show off during rutting season. The crash of their opposing charges could be heard for miles, echoing off the mountainsides with the resounding force of the desert's largest land-based mammals. But a female bighorn? It most likely would have been a defensive situation, maybe with her offspring. Or maybe a mishap, caught in a narrow place? Or a fall? But he had never seen a bighorn slip as they stepped high on narrow ledges with sure-footed confidence. No, the damaged appendage was most likely the result of a stalwart defense rather than a mishap or aggression, he felt.

Haberman and the ewe watched each other for almost a minute. Then she was startled by something, stepped over the crest of the ridge, and was gone. He knew that the other side of the mountain received more rain, and was a little more green with foliage. The bighorn would favor that eastern slope for food, water, and shelter. The claim was on the rocky leeward side of the mountain, which received the wind-driven storms from the west.

Sailors are aware of the lee shore, and wary, as the wind

against the shore might force a boat aground, or shatter it on the rocks. On most of the Pacific islands where Haberman had sailed, the leeward shore was drier and rockier than the windward side. In the Hawaiian territory, the lee shore was the west and south face of each island. It was similar here in the mountains. Most of this desert received only a few inches of rain each year, but those few inches could be densely concentrated in time and space.

During this time of year, most of the dark clouds rolled in from the west, and they frequently passed over the leeward slope without bursting into rain, scattering only sparse cool drops on the rocks and dry washes. Then the clouds could pause and shroud the peaks for minutes, hours, or days, glowering and sometimes raining, but mostly just thundering before moving windward. Then the bulk of the storm might let loose. Or more frequently, the clouds would move on through the mountain range and across the valleys to the east without erupting in rain at all. This was called a rain shadow, and it was a shadow within the larger rain shadow of the transverse ranges that included Mount San Gorgonio. When the storms finally drifted east, the sun could emerge very quickly, and this side of the mountain would bask in its normal shine.

He paused for a moment and looked at the ore cart that was almost full. He had lately noticed something else about the lee shore of these mountains. Most of the more lucrative mines had been on a leeward slope, like the Desert Queen and the Lost Horse. Some of the less productive mines, like the Anaconda, were on the windward side. For this and a few other specific reasons, Haberman thought this claim to the east was extremely promising. On Thursday, he had mixed a couple hundred pounds of this new ore with a load from the Anaconda. Keane had remarked, "Joe, this must be the richest ore that we've ever milled for you. Is it really from the Anaconda?"

Haberman had picked up one of the gold mattes, and felt the satisfying heft. "Well, it's from more than one location, Ry. I think I'm ready to send this bullion to Sacramento." The next ore taken to Keane's Mill would have even more rocks from this claim, and it would likely be a rich one. Though they had occasional disagreements and friction, he trusted Ryland Keane to be honest in his dealings. Though Keane had earned some quick-draw notoriety in situations with no surviving witnesses, Haberman felt that he was a man of integrity in his way, true to his own code. He never heard Keane gossiping about the value of any particular ore that came through the mill, no more than a banker would gab about a depositor's balance or assets.

Stan returned from the truck with an empty ore cart ready to be loaded. Haberman told him, "We're crackin' some good-looking ore, young man. Things are looking up for us." Stan grinned and nodded his head, and they started shoveling ore into the cart without another word. Haberman smiled again to himself. This is the most steady-working crew I've ever had, he thought. He felt strong and healthy, and took a deep breath of the mountain air as he stood the shovel against a boulder. He exhaled. Taking the pick in hand, he took another swing at the rock wall of the recessed area, breaking off a nice chunk.

The bighorn ewe lifted her nose to the breeze. She had picked up the odor of the coyote without seeing him. She calmly turned her head and strolled over to a granite wall that was almost sheer, but not quite. Moving from a ledge to a crack to the next subtle foothold, she scaled the wall in a nimble zig-zag, and reached the next plateau before the coyote knew her exact location. She moved on without looking back, knowing that the coyote couldn't scale the wall. He would have to backtrack to find an easier but much longer route to the plateau. It was unlikely that he would expend the effort, especially since a lone coyote had very little chance of bringing down an adult bighorn.

The chase and escape were almost a daily game to her and the coyotes. Unless she made a mistake, or was impaired by injury or poor health, she could always get away. She had eluded this particular coyote several times in the past, and her parents had eluded this coyote's parents and grandparents in these same mountains. She looked around at the slopes below, having left the coyote behind, and began chew on a tuft of grass, not as green as she would like, but still nutritious enough to fuel another rock scramble or two.

12

Breakfast

Smoothed by orbicular grinding over time, the center was a seasoned circle, a lighter shade of gray than the rest of the *molcajete*, which had been carved and shaped from a single chunk of basalt. William Quine emptied a small paper bag of almonds onto the spot, chopped them, and then crushed them with circular force. He used the *tejolote* to grind the almond pieces into a powder, and then mixed the almond meal in a ceramic bowl with mesquite flour from a separate bag. There was a large chip on the rim of the bowl, which reduced its capacity only slightly.

The *molcajete*, fully intact, was a convenient, indoor version of the grinding *morteros* he had seen in bedrock throughout the area, frequently near caves, fire rings, and other signs of native gathering places. The *morteros* were of various diameters and depths to grind natural ingredients for food, medicine, cleansing, and ceremony. His grandfather had told him about mesquite cakes, consumed for hundreds of years, made from mesquite pods milled to flour by resolute grinding. Other *morteros* might be used to grind pine nuts or chia seeds to mix with the mesquite flour. He had added several other ingredients, most local except for a couple imports that he used when they were available and affordable: bananas and cinnamon, which made the mesquite cakes even more delicious.

He thought back to the time his grandfather had crushed some chia seeds in a bedrock *mortero* when they were walking in the mountains together, late in one of the summers of William's boyhood. Grandfather had told William the Chemehuevi word for grinding an ingredient in a *mortero*, and described its meaning in a way that was similar to the English word "activate" but a little different. William had only heard that word once, when he was eight years old and spending rare time with his grandfather, and he could not remember it now.

But when he used the *molcajete*, he considered it to be more than merely grinding something, but also a way to activate a food or herb's special properties as a healing agent. He believed that his state of mind and intentions while grinding could have an effect on the ingredient.

The crushing, grinding, and mixing were all done quietly. It was seven a.m., and he thought that someone might still be sleeping. A month earlier, he had rented a room in this house where his cousins and their extended families lived, on the southern outskirts of Twentynine Palms, not far from the oasis that had been one of the ancestral homes of the Serrano and Chemehuevi people of the Morongo Basin.

His two distant cousins and their wives, along with their kids, had risen before dawn to attend services at the Catholic church in San Bernardino. All six of them had crammed into an old Plymouth, the men and boys in ties, and the women in their Sunday dresses. William expected them to return in the afternoon. "We'll bring you lunch if you let us have a dozen of your mesquite cakes," his cousin Erwin had suggested, and William agreed. He would have given them some cakes, and had done so more than once. But Erwin liked to bargain, and he liked to give something back in return for the cakes.

When William had arrived in Twentynine Palms a couple months earlier, returning for the first time since childhood, he had been looking forward to being reunited with family members of Native origin. But he was disappointed to find that few of them were interested in their heritage and the old ways, other than a liking for his mesquite treats. Most of the household had only one Native grandparent or great-grandparent, and they had become almost entirely assimilated with the growing numbers of homesteaders, miners, cattlemen, and other desert seekers. But they took a liking to Quine, who at twenty-seven was about the same age as the couples, and they welcomed him into the household. They respected his Navy service and seafaring experience as well as his general seriousness and work habits.

The main part of the house was adobe, and there were additions on three sides, built with reinforced cinder blocks and finished with stucco to resemble adobe. His room was a small annex that had been intended to store wood and outdoor tools. They had moved the wood to a shed, but there was still a few rakes and shovels at the end of his cot. Today he would use different tools.

On Sunday mornings, by agreement with the household, he was allowed to use the kitchen in the main part of the house. The stove/oven was powered by propane, and Quine had purchased the full tank that was attached and flowing. On the stove top, a pot simmered. He lifted the lid and used a wooden spoon to stir the mix, a few handfuls of chopped and pitted dates with a couple cups of water. It had started to darken and thicken into a slurry with a sweet fragrance, which meant it was ready. He turned off the burner and took the pot off the stove. Then he added a scoop of baking soda to the mix, which foamed and lightened as he stirred. He put the lid back on the pot, off-center so it would cool slightly while he mixed the other ingredients separately. He turned on the oven to preheat.

Mesquite cakes could contain a variety of grains, nuts, fruits, and berries, depending on what was fresh and available. He felt some confidence that the assortment of ingredients in this batch would be delicious. Dates had become more available in recent years, obtained in trade from the Cahuilla in the lower desert, or sometimes purchased there. In the right storage conditions, they seemed to last longer than any other fresh fruit. To Quine, they provided a unique flavor and sweetness, and were his favorite added ingredient. The flavors of the dates, nuts, and mesquite would combine and synergize while baking, enhanced by cinnamon, an import that seemed exotic to some.

The traditional way of cooking would have been over a fire, or in a stone oven. But Quine liked the measured heat of this propane appliance. Mesquite flour, as an ingredient, would usually start to burn at about 375 degrees Fahrenheit, so he was careful with the temperature. Some people liked it a little burnt and blackened, and they said it tasted like chocolate. Quine aimed to preserve the balance of subtle flavors by not burning the cakes. He scooped batter into the cups of the muffin pan, and topped them with walnut pieces. Then he put the pans in the oven, and he glanced at the wind-up clock built into the "deluxe" stove. The cakes would be ready in about twenty minutes.

He stepped out the back door. Sparrows and finches were chirping in a creosote ring that crossed the property line. Quine walked over to sit on a flat rock at the other edge of the yard, in front of another creosote abuzz with tiny yellow flowers. In the mid-morning Sunday lull, he could hear the faint buzz from bees on the other side of the bush, sampling the blossoms while oh-by-the-way pollinating. The slightest of breezes stirred, then stopped, then whispered through the bushes and across his bare arms. A hedgehog cactus was blooming in purple at the base of an old stone wall.

Suddenly Quine was aware of a noiseless change in air pressure near his right ear, and a Cooper's Hawk streaked by his head into the yard in front of him. Intensely focused and lightning fast, the hawk tried to grab a dove in his talons but missed. While the hawk had been in flight behind Quine, the yard birds had been unaware, seeing Quine but maybe not looking beyond him. But when the hawk appeared from behind Quine and quickened towards them, the doves had a split-second to warn and fly, and the songbirds and rabbits scattered.

After the hawk missed the dove and landed in the sand, he paused and remained motionless near a rock with identical coloration. A couple of dove feathers began to move with the wind across the yard. The hawk would wait here, conserving energy, and shortly a blithe songbird might alight, not seeing the hawk. Like many animals including humans, the hawk could camouflage strategically, though it wasn't one of his primary weapons.

Quine remained motionless also. The hawk would probably

fly away, uneasy, if Quine moved or made noise, and he was already aware of the human presence. Hawks were uncomfortable with people, who had no place in their food pyramid. To the hawk, humans were neither hunter nor hunted; merely strange and difficult to evaluate. Quine watched the hawk, and in his mind said to himself, *"keyek-keyek."* That was the Serrano name for this kind of hawk, known for streaking through clearings and yards, wheeling around bushes and trees, turning with a dip of the wing, talons flexing, a silent terror to its prey.

Anyone who kept chickens was aware of this raptor, and some called it a "chicken hawk." He preferred *keyek-keyek*, as that locution had a shape like the flight of this hawk in its low arc around a mesquite ring, first in one direction and then another with talons ready. The middle of each word seemed to pivot smoothly around the letter *'y'* like the hawk in its curvilinear flight.

He thought about the native words that he knew, which were more than a few. But most of the words were terms for animals, plants, or places, and he couldn't connect them with verbs and the other building blocks of a sentence. His native words were like a collection of interesting objects on separate pedestals that never interacted or came to life. Daily usage of native words had been frowned upon in school, and his cousins and housemates didn't know the native tongues either. But Quine savored the words he knew, spoke them with pride, and wanted to learn more. He wanted to hear conversations and participate easily, to make jokes and tell stories.

The *keyek-keyek* suddenly used his powerful talons to spring into the air while he spread and then flapped his wings, and he flew into a wooded area a short distance away, where a rabbit screamed. Breakfast. Quine realized that the mesquite cakes were probably ready, and he went back to the kitchen, which radiated an inviting aroma.

13

The Blacksmith

William opened the screen door and stepped into the kitchen. He avoided the creaking spot on the floor, even though the only one near enough to hear was Goldie, an older dog of mixed breeds including golden retriever. She slept soundly but not soundlessly below the kitchen table. The linoleum was a checkerboard pattern of red and beige, but the red had faded to a coral hue over the decades. With its large, south-facing windows, the kitchen was the brightest room in the house, and frequently the busiest.

He pulled an oven mitt onto each hand and removed one hot pan, then the other, to the kitchen counter. The room had a warmly aromatic personality of mesquite and cinnamon. He removed the mitts and turned off the oven. Using a butter knife, he pried loose a couple of hot cakes, placed them on a cloth napkin, then pulled out a chair and sat down.

He looked at the cakes, roughly the size and shape of small muffins, and then he picked one up and took a bite. He enjoyed the combination of flavors, cinnamon and mesquite leading the parade, then the sweet dates and bananas with the crunch of walnuts and a hint of chia. He felt that they were usually better on the second day after baking, but they were hard to resist when they were fresh from the oven.

William ate the cake in two bites even though it was hot, and then he heard familiar sounds outside approaching the door. Sounded like Jesse, but was he carrying something?

Yes, he had taken off his backpack and was lugging it at his side up to the door. William stood to help, but Jesse held up his hand in a halting gesture. "I can get it." He took a nimble step over the creak spot, which stayed silent, and while still looking at the floor, said to William, "Ha. Foiled the burglar alarm again."

William smiled, and said, "I guess Goldie's not the alarm any more. Have a mesquite cake."

Jesse replied, "Thanks, the mesquite aroma carried me through the door." He set his backpack on a kitchen chair. "And thanks for paying your rent on time again, William." Jesse had owned the house for decades, and knew William's grandfather before he passed. He untied and loosened the draw string of the backpack, then reached inside and took out a paper bag. "Found some curly dock!" he said triumphantly.

"Curly dock?" asked William.

"Some people call it wild rhubarb," said Jesse. He took several leaves from the bag. "The wide green ones taste different than the young leaves. But both need to be cooked."

"I'm done with the stove and oven."

"We'll have a feast today. Scrambled eggs and peppers with some curly dock, sauteed. With your top-notch mesquite cakes, plus whatever they bring back from San Bernardino," said Jesse.

"Where does curly dock grow around here?"

"With the drought, it's been harder to find. I went to two

places where it didn't sprout at all this season. I had to go to a spot in the mountains where three washes meet, so a rainfall triples in its flow there. Curly dock needs more than a sprinkle to pop up and sprout." Jesse separated the leaves on the cutting board.

"I'll grind some chia and pepper for it," said William.

"Good idea," replied Jesse. "Chia brings endurance. It was one of the helpers that Willie Boy cooperated to outrun that posse and their horses."

"I heard some things about that," said William, glancing up at Jesse. "I guess there's another side to the story that's different from the newspapers."

"That's right. The posse shot Carlota. Willy didn't. And when they finally showed Willy's dead body in the newspaper, with that picture shot from twenty feet away and the head turned, well, that wasn't Willy."

"I was a kid living in a foster home then," said William. "Before I went to Sherman."

"They wanted to make the Natives look violent, to help justify rounding them up on reservations. Your relatives at the Oasis of Mara had to move, not long after that."

"How did they lose the land?" asked William.

"One day, about twenty years ago, strangers showed up with a piece of paper that said they owned that land. White people with paper, and the sheriff was there to enforce. The Serrano and Chemehuevi didn't have that piece of paper, even though they had been there for generations." said Jesse.

"How'd you keep your place?"

"I have a deed. The Indian Agent only came to my door once. I'm 25% Paiute, the rest is German, Dutch, and English," replied Jesse. "I was also the only blacksmith in town at the time, so nobody wanted me to move."

"I thought you were at least half Native," said William.

Jesse half-smiled. "You might call me a quarter-breed. But we didn't think too much about percentages and quanta until those Indian Agents came around. I spent a lot of time with the Chemehuevi and Serrano back when they were at Mara, and elsewhere in Twentynine Palms. Your grandfather was one of my best friends, rest in peace."

William recalled his grandfather talking and joking with Jesse here in this same kitchen, years ago, and he smiled too.

Jesse looked up at William, and said, "You remember when he took you out of Sherman and brought you here for a few days? In the summer?"

"Very well," replied William. "When I was ten, and then the next summer when I was eleven. You let us sleep in your bedroom, the coolest room," he gestured toward the northeast corner of the house, "And you slept in the add-on where I'm staying now."

"That's a good sleeping room if no rakes or shovels fall into your bed," said Jesse, smiling and thinking of the various implements that hung on the walls.

William chuckled. "I rehung most of those on the opposite wall. I can sleep at the Anaconda cabin too, but I like it better here."

Jesse started cracking some eggs into a bowl. "How's the Anaconda? You like going down into that mine?"

"Well, I don't really like it that much, but it's interesting sometimes, and I'm earning a living."

"I guess there were some miners on your father's side of the family. Never knew him. Your mother's side was the opposite of miners. They were mountain climbers and trail runners with their heads touching the clouds," said Jesse.

"I try to honor both sides," said William.

Jesse was silent for a moment, thinking of how to phrase a remark about William's father. He said instead, "These newcomers give status to the ones who accumulate the most. The Natives respect the ones who do the most for other people, like the healers, and the hunters who feed the children and elders. I see you stepping on that road, like when you make these mesquite cakes with new ingredients, then give them away," he said, looking in William's direction with a serious expression.

"Thanks, Jesse," said William. He paused for a moment, then asked, "What do you remember about my grandmother and the Serrano around here?"

"Your grandmother Iris was a gracious woman and a great cook. She was not tall, but she was a beautiful dancer."

"Do you remember when she and my grandfather were courting?"

"I was in the Army during that time, in the peacetime cavalry. That's where I learned to be a blacksmith. When I finally came back here, they were married with a young girl, your mother."

"Did you know my mother?"

"Not well." He paused for a moment, and a shadow crossed his face. William had the impression that he wasn't telling everything he knew. "I never lived at the Oasis, and those were busy years at the shop. We kept the forge hot all day long."

"What were the Serrano people around here like? In their heyday?"

"Their heyday? Well, that was a few generations before I got here, before smallpox and relocations and conversions and so forth. 'Serrano' was what the Spanish missionaries called them.

It was their name for mountaineers," said Jesse.

"I remember what you said way back when, about their name for themselves: *Maarenga'yam,* the people of Morongo. I was sitting on a straw mat at your church."

"You remember that? Those were the years I was still teaching Sunday School."

"You're teaching me some Sunday School right now."

Jesse smiled wryly. "I had to stop teaching on Sundays at the church. I shared perspectives from more than one group of people, and the new minister didn't like that."

"I told some other kids at Sherman about the *Maarenga'yam.*" said William.

Jesse smiled. "Good. The *Maarenga'yam* got along well with almost everyone, except maybe the Mohave. Many other Native travelers came through here on trading missions, mostly east and west to the ocean and back, but sometimes south to the gulf and then back north."

"Most of the mountain passes around here aren't very obvious from a distance."

"The transverse ranges are tricky. Travelers needed guides. The Serrano could show them mountain passes and water sources, heal them with desert medicine, and trade them pine nuts, mesquite, chia, and more. They could feed them with venison and mesquite cakes like yours." He smiled.

"They probably could trade for sea salt, shells, and dried fish from the coastal people. Sometimes the Sherman students traded with each other like that," said William.

"An old friend passed through here with sea salt a while back," said Jesse. "Still have some." He stood, opened a cupboard door, and took out a small jar of amber glass.

"Weren't there a lot of people around here with both Serrano and Chemehuevi blood, like me?"

"Oh, yes. There were many intermarriages. When the Chemehuevi crossed the Colorado many generations back, they became even closer to the Serrano, who were never large in number. Before they came over, it was getting hard for Serranos to find unrelated people to marry."

"How closely related were Willy and Carlota for their marriage to be disallowed?" asked William.

"I heard that they were five degrees of kinship apart. The elder relatives knew who beget who, and they laid out pebbles in the sand. One row for each generation, and they figured it out."

William thought for a moment, and said, "A visual representation of the oral tradition."

Jesse smiled. "That's right. You've made yourself into a thinking man. Your grandfather would be proud."

"Thanks, Jesse," said William, blushing internally. "Help yourself to another mesquite cake or two."

"Gladly," said Jesse, reaching for another cake.

"You know, I've been thinking," said William.

"I thought so," smiled Jesse.

"People say that the Natives didn't have a written culture. And it's true that we didn't write words on paper like the Europeans or the Egyptians," stated William. He looked at Jesse across the table.

"Go on," replied Jesse, still smiling.

"Writing words on paper is one way of representing abstract ideas in the physical world. But our Native cultures came up with other ways to do it," said William.

"Yes, using objects from the natural world. Arranging pebbles in rows can tell you the same things as a genealogical chart. But what other ways can you name?" asked Jesse.

"Well, there are petroglyphs and pictographs on rocks, of course," said William. "But most of the meanings have been lost over time."

"We still remember the petroglyphs that were used as a solar calendar. With the sunbeams hitting certain lines on the solstices, equinoxes, and midpoints. I'll see if I can take you to a Chemehuevi ceremony on the solstice. And introduce you to some people at the reservation here at the base of the mountain."

"I'd like that a lot," said William, who looked at his spoons and mixing bowls in the sink, and he felt like he should be washing them, but wanted to talk to Jesse more. "What about a lunar calendar?"

"Oh, that's a good one," said Jesse. "See that tortoise shell hanging on the wall? That young tortoise was overturned and eaten by ravens."

William looked at the shell as if he was seeing it for the first time.

"You probably thought it was used as a mixing bowl, and I've done that a time or two," said Jesse. "But it's also a lunar calendar."

"Hmm. How does that work?" asked William.

"Notice that there are thirteen plates, which they call scutes, in the center of the shell."

"Yes."

"Then if you count the smaller segments going 'round the margin of the shell, there are twenty-eight of those."

"Why didn't I notice that? Thirteen moons in a year, and twenty-eight days for each moon," replied William.

Jesse stopped chopping curly dock, and put down the knife.

"On the tortoise shell calendar, time is circular, not linear." He pointed at one of the large center scutes at the top of the shell. "This would be the first moon of the year, and the lunar New Year's Day would be this little square on the margin, at the top."

William studied the tortoise shell for a moment, letting his eyes follow the orbit of time. The days were a circle, and the months were a spiral. "Where are we today?" he asked.

"Well, some nations measure from New Moon to New Moon, and others start the month on the Full Moon. That's how I do it. We are on the twentieth day of the fourth lunar month," he said as he pointed with one hand at the month scute, and the other at a rim square at the edge of the shell. "But on the Gregorian solar calendar, with no tortoises, it's April 10, 1932."

"Okay, but 28 times 13 equals 364," said William. "Where do you get the extra day to match the solar year?"

Jesse smiled. "Good point. There would be one day a year that wasn't on the lunar calendar. Maybe that was a day of rest."

"Maybe it was a day of rest for the tortoises too. They didn't have to work as a calendar!" said William.

Jesse laughed. "Yes, a holiday for humans and tortoises both." He picked up the knife and resumed chopping the curly dock.

"When do you think they'll get back from San Bernardino?" asked William, thinking of his cousins and their families.

"Mid-afternoon, probably about two or three," replied Jesse.

"I might try to get in a nap before they get here," said William, thinking of the shady hammock in the backyard.

"Me too," said Jesse, thinking of his cool bedroom and a quiet house.

Horned lizards use the bony extrusions of their foreheads for the same purposes that bighorn rams or barnyard bulls jut and jab with their horns. The lizard will employ tactics that are similar to how a seal or walrus uses its tusks. Might the lizard's horns be some form of cartilage or skin, you ask? No, the lizard has true horns, with a solid bone core encased in a sheath of keratin. It has been speculated that this outer layer of the lizard's horns is as fully sensate as the singular tusk of a narwhal.

This lizard uses its horns to defend itself against predators, and within its own species to tussle for dominance and in disputes. If you were near enough in the quiet desert, you might hear the clash of two lizards' horns in combat, similar to the crash of bighorn sheep but without the amplifications of size, muscle, and echo.

Buried in soft sand, the horned lizard situates its head so that it can still breathe and hear. When an ant walks within a few inches of its nose, the lizard leaps, chomps, and swallows the ant: another successful meal for the small reptile that has been called "horny toad" affectionately by generations of active kids.

On the sand and rock of the desert, the horned lizard can disappear into its context. If approached, it may become motionless and rely on this camouflage, or it may try to dash quickly and then stop. It seeks to merge into the pattern of its chosen spot. To a predator, the lizard has two speeds: one hectic, the other frozen. If caught, its horns, ridges, and scales will hinder swallowing and digestion; a snake may spit it out in disgust after several minutes of discomfort. When necessary, a horned lizard can defend itself by squirting blood from its eyes.

William was relaxing in the backyard hammock, listening to the songbirds, when his cousin's car pulled in the driveway, and parked near the house. Erwin and his wife Judy stepped out, along with their two young sons and another adult couple related to Judy. The six of them moved towards the kitchen door. William was there first, and opened it.

"Welcome back. How were the roads?"

"They were all in good shape," replied Erwin. "We had an interesting lunch in Berdoo." He placed some paper bags on the table, which had been expanded with an extra leaf for the Sunday meals.

William took a bag from the cupboard, bulky with mesquite cakes, and gave it to Erwin. Then he brought out a plateful and sat it on the table.

The children immediately grabbed cakes with enthusiasm. "Slow down, kids, and mind your manners," said Erwin. "What do you say to Uncle William?"

"Thanks, Uncle William!" "Thanks, Uncle!" He wasn't their uncle, exactly, but he liked being called that.

"Our Sunday potlucks sure improved since you came around with these mesquite cakes," said Judy.

"Thanks, Judy," said William. "Did you find someplace good to eat after church?"

"We went to a restaurant where they pass your food through a window and you never even go inside!" said their precocious young son, Rico. "There were long lines but they moved fast."

Jesse appeared in the doorway. "Well, how was the food?" He sat down at the head of the table.

"Good, Uncle Jesse! We brought some for you and William," said Rico, putting down his mesquite cake and opening one of the paper bags on the table. "They make these hamburgers on big trays, rows and rows all at once." He took out a couple of items wrapped in thin paper, and passed one to Jesse, and one to William.

William unwrapped it and looked it over. He had eaten hamburgers before, but they weren't like this. He peeled off the top bun. The meat patty was strangely uniform, perfectly round, but thin. The condiments were bright primary or secondary colors, like toys made for toddlers. The ketchup was a splat of red, the mustard a jarring yellow, and the pickle an iridescent green.

He reassembled the burger, and took a bite. The bun had no flavor at all. The meat was gristly and vague. The ketchup was too sweet, and didn't taste like tomato. The mustard, like all the other elements of the sandwich, had only a single taste, without subtlety or complexity. He liked the pickle more than any other ingredient, but he had consumed better pickles.

William put the hamburger down, and saw that the families had scattered, adults to their rooms to change out of their church clothes, and kids to the backyard, happily rambunctious. He looked over at Jesse, who had taken only two bites of his burger. Jesse looked at William, then picked his burger up again, and passed it under the table to the dog Goldie, who gulped it down. After a moment, William did the same.

14

The Sermon

In a stark valley east of Twentynine Palms, a road of soft sand crossed a less-traveled road of softer sand, loose and grainy like a beach above the highwater line. A tumbleweed moved fitfully across the landscape, detached from one snag and on the way to another. A lone ant carried a tidbit back to his commune.

The sun was an hour beyond its zenith, and the Church of the Desert Nazarene was in session. The small room was crowded and warm, and open windows on the east and west provided very little cross-draft. A year earlier, the Reverend had attached a wooden steeple to the peaked roof of his two-room cabin, and began delivering twice-weekly sermons in the main room. If you happened to be passing by, and glanced in a window on this Sunday afternoon, you would see fourteen congregants of various ages and backgrounds. A young couple in clean, mended clothes sat on a wooden bench, attentive but frequently distracted. On a faded, homespun rug at their feet, their three toddlers sat and fidgeted, their legs alternately crossed and splayed. A middle-aged couple sat together on another bench, which might have resembled a pew if it had a back. With a diversity of creed and temperament, there were five unattached people scattered on wooden chairs, including Joe Haberman. Two bachelors stood with their hats in hand, leaning against the wall near the door, ready to escape on short notice. One of the seated congregants, a younger man with blond hair, leaned his chair back on two legs, enjoyed the reclining angle for a moment, then thought better of it and returned to rectitude, with all four chair legs and his own bipedal extremities flat on the floor.

Mid-sermon, the Reverend paused, raised his eyebrows, and inquired of the congregation, "Can you tell me which bird or beast, of all the flying, crawling, and trotting things, was most reluctant to join Noah's Ark?" He paused for a beat, then answered himself. "It was the buzzard. Some call it a vulture. They eat dead things, which were likely to be found in great quantity in the flood outside the boat, but not on it. The ark was of course a place of blessed abundant life, each species coupled and seeded with eternity. The vultures, being seekers and consumers of death and disease, would most assuredly be outcasts among the vivacious couples of abundant life. But the vulture plays an important role in the grand scheme of things, as necessary as any other. They rank highly among the sanctified agents of material decomposition. Just as the Creator sees every sparrow's fall, he also sees the rise of the buzzard in the warming air currents of the sky, searching for the fallen sparrow."

He looked out the window as if he saw a vulture there, but there were none, and the day had become sunny and clear after a gray dawn. His face at the window had the expression of an open, trusting person who had become more cautious as decades passed. Between sentences, his mouth was a firm line of deliberation, but there were smile lines like parentheses at the corners of his mouth. He continued, "There was a crow's nest on the ark, a place for a sailor to access the topsail and see for a distance. Then above the crow's nest, there was another crows' nest for the actual crows to nest. Above that, there was a nest for the ravens, and then there were nests for albatrosses, various hawks, falcons, and eagles at the top."

His gaze scanned the congregation quickly, looking directly into the eyes of one attendee and then another. He paused at Haberman, whose eyes looked watery and haunted. It was not an unusual look in this desert. Then the Reverend continued. "But there was no place for the vulture in this masted hierarchy of winged things. They were different from the others. Some might consider the vulture to be the lowest of the low, but in their own way, they were equal to the eagles. They were apart from the ark, though near it, and if they were to rest at all, it would be on flotsam or carrion afloat. Then, after resting, they would flap their wings vigorously to catch up, and they would fly above the swimming creatures of the sea in their ordained pairs, including several species of whales in the grand armada of leviathans. The vulture couple usually flew behind the others, but above and apart too. They were holy outcasts."

After the service, the Captain drove westward towards the Anaconda. He decided to detour onto Copper Mountain, west of Twentynine Palms. As a commodity, copper was not of great value at the moment, but he had staked a claim for its future potential. A winding road had been cut and graded from the rock, in some places a narrow shelf on the mountainside, with a couple of side paths down canyons. He kept on the main course until he suddenly slowed and stopped.

On the road ahead, a snake was moving slowly, crossing from left to right without haste, absorbing warmth from the sand and late afternoon sun. Haberman halted the truck with plenty of space between himself and the snake. He stepped out to look it over, and saw that it was a speckled rattlesnake, probably the most commonly seen rattler in this desert. Even though Haberman was about thirty feet away, the snake stopped crossing to rattle a warning, loudly and clearly, like maracas he had heard in his travels, and continuous.

"Thank you for the music, Mr. Rattler," said Haberman. "Your rhythm is good, but I like some melody in the song." The snake looked at Haberman, and saw that he wasn't coming any closer. He slithered to the road's edge and into the underbrush, rattling all the while. The Captain liked speckled rattlesnakes because they usually gave plenty of warning, unlike sidewinders that might be coiled in the sand, almost hidden. He spoke in a playful, teasing tone to animals that he liked, which were most of them. He cursed at ones he despised, like the Mojave rattlesnake, bees, wasps, cowbirds, and the annoying sand gnats.

The Captain sang to the rhythm of the rattle. "There's treasure in the hills, and music in the hearts of men." He was in a cheerful mood, buoyed by the hymns that had been sung after the sermon. The snake disappeared into the brush, and stopped rattling. Haberman returned to his truck, and resumed his drive home to the tent cabin at the Anaconda.

15

Surmises

William and Jem began driving to Bonanza Springs in the last pitch of darkness before day began. The breeze, though dry, had a cool touch. Most of the roads were better than expected, especially the recently paved segment of Route 66 that jutted northeast towards the Clipper Mountains. The sun began to assert itself, first with a glow, then a shaft of light and another, then fully illuminating the landscape to declare the day. They both pulled their caps down over their right temples to shield the rising sun, and William took a brief nap in the passenger seat while Jem drove the truck. They had been assigned a day's work at the Captain's most distant claim, about a mile beyond the spring that was their first stop.

They parked on a flat spot a short distance away from the two green lines of bending willows, half-grown mesquites, and cottonwoods busy with songbirds. Between the trees were long grasses and reeds, and the springs. Everyone who passed through the area refreshed their canteens and containers at Bonanza, which flowed with many gallons of visible water, one of the most generous springs in the Mojave. It was known by every species for a hundred miles and more. Now Jem was kneeling in the shade next to a deep puddle, refilling and saturating the burlap water bag that usually hung on the truck's radiator. The new day was still around 70° F, but it might rise to 90° at this altitude in mid-afternoon, a few degrees warmer than Twentynine Palms. Jem reattached the water bag to the truck's grill, then grabbed his canteen, walked back to the spring, and filled it while William was doing the same. They both drank deeply.

After refilling and refreshing, they found themselves lingering beyond the spring. They stood and stretched beside the truck, hesitating, breathing in the morning air. Then one and then the other sat on the shaded running board, where Jem started peeling an orange, and William took out a coffee can that was full of mesquite cakes. They traded cakes and oranges without discussion, and ate breakfast with their eyes drawn to the green oasis at the springs, drinking with their vision while they ate. The rest of the day would be spent in the brown and beige hills beyond the oasis, dry.

William thought back to his days in the Navy, when a lush green island would appear on the horizon, visible from a distance when the sun was shining and the sky was clear. An oasis in the desert is like an island to a sailor, he thought. More than a landmark, necessary for life. Oases, islands, and springs were specifically marked on maps ever since the first map was scrawled in the sand with a stick, one person telling another, "There is water to drink here, and probably food." William looked across the rifted and ridgy desert, and in his mind the desert became an ocean for a second, then returned to sand and rock. The breeze felt warmer now.

Jem was thinking of the night before, when he had been invited to dinner at Palmhaven Cabins with Ned and his sisters, Lee and Alma. He thought now of the younger sister, Alma, who had sat beside him under the palm trees at the picnic table for much of the evening. They had talked together about various things in the desert and in the world, but now he recalled that even her quietest words had a musical quality that was like bells ringing, a sound of shimmering roundness in the air, and he remembered that quality more than her specific words. Looking into her round, hazel eyes, she seemed a constellation of pleasant spheres and circles, with her round, open face in the moonlight. The music of her voice echoed around his mind.

William and Jem finished eating about the same time, and both stood up and looked in each direction. Then they got in the truck. Jem started it and shifted into gear.

"Still haven't seen any of those red-spotted toads," said William.

"Me neither," replied Jem.

16

The Tail

Joshua trees can reach more than forty feet tall, beckoning and gesticulating to the sky like prophets, but their roots in the desert sand are surprisingly shallow. Even the largest and most ancient Joshuas extend only a few feet deep into the cryptobiotic. One of the leading causes of death in mature Joshua trees is a fatal fall to the ground, a result of their top-heavy nature.

After living for hundreds of years, a stalwart Joshua tree might have an animal burrow near its roots, weakening their hold. A rain might soften the soil, and then strong winds, reaching 50 miles per hour or more, can be the toppler. In some Joshua tree woodlands, as many as one of every ten Joshua tree trunks is in a horizontal state. Not infrequently, a segment of the roots remains in the ground, and the tree produces flowers and fruits for many seasons while in a recumbent position. In the fallen trees that are entirely dead, decomposition can take decades in the dry desert air, and some animals and insects have evolved to use the decaying trunks for habitats and hunting.

For several species of lizards, particularly the desert night lizard, a favorite shelter is under fallen Joshua trees and yuccas, where they can dig burrows, and live in extended families that might reach a dozen or more. The Joshua trunk is heavier than you might expect if you, the reader, tried to lift it in the same casual way that you pick up this book or device. It is also too heavy for coyotes, foxes, bobcats, or other predators to dislodge. The trunk-roofed burrow provides the lizards shelter from the sun and wind, and is less arid than the open air. The decaying trunks and surrounding areas are populated by beetles, termites, ants, crickets, grasshoppers, and other favorite foods of lizards.

Side-blotched lizards hunt the same prey as night lizards, but they usually shelter in rock crevices or other animals' abandoned burrows rather than under Joshua trunks. But the female side-blotched lizard, in particular, likes to sun herself on a Joshua log, and maybe eat an insect or two if they come near. The male side-blotched lizard, in his most common morph, has different markings, speckled rather than striped, which camouflage well on bare sand or monzogranite. The female's markings are better suited for camouflage in grass and twig areas, or the shaggy top of a fallen Joshua trunk. These dissimilar markings allow a side-blotched lizard couple to hunt or bask while camouflaged on different surfaces in the same area.

On this evening, a female side-blotched lizard enjoys the gentle rays of the fading sunlight. Though pattern-matched on a fibrously decomposed Joshua log, she has been spotted from above. A loggerhead shrike, perched at the top of a nearby Joshua tree, watches her with intensity and intent.

The loggerhead shrike is a songbird that hunts like a raptor, and can hover like a hummingbird. A shrike will sit for long minutes at the top of a Joshua tree, sometimes voicing its turf-claiming song if near the border, but mostly watching for movement on the sand below. They are well-dispersed in the desert, with territories up to forty acres for a shrike couple.

With such capacious hunting grounds, a shrike has not ventured into this particular group of Joshuas for some time. This shrike is not recognized as a threat by the lizard, being perceived as a songbird in size, form, and musicality. The shrike does not have the hooked beak or predatory gaze of a hawk or falcon, and does not have their razor-sharp talons. His eyes and the direction of his gaze might not be discerned by the lizard, as the shrike's eyes are black within the black mask.

A shrike spends much of the day perched in overlooking places, on a boulder or in a tree, relaxed but alert. The small animals, insects, and other prey of interest to the shrike will eventually move between brush and bush across the desert sand, with motions seen from above. When the time and angle are right, the shrike will dive and try to talon-grasp the prey at each end. If they succeed, they will carry the victim a short distance and impale it on a Joshua spike, sharp branch, barbed wire, cactus spine, or other skewer-like object. There it can be butchered and consumed at leisure with aplomb.

On this day, the shrike sees the lizard scamper from some blackbrush scrub to the fallen Joshua tree. He watches every move as she climbs to an optimally camouflaged place on the log. She stops there, stays motionless, and begins to thermoregulate in the gentle oblique of the setting sun.

At the top of the tree, the shrike is also motionless, un-watched by the side-blotched lizard after a cursory glance. With half-lidded eyes, the lizard basks on the log for some moments, and then the shrike dives suddenly, silently, and she doesn't start to flee until he is only a couple feet away. The lizard scrambles down to the ground with speed almost equal to the shrike, but not quite, and he hovers above her escape path and then strikes, reaching for her neck and tail. The lizard twists her torso just so, and the shrike's left talon grabs sand. His right talon grasps the tail just below its base, and she contracts the muscles at the base of the tail to detach it, while held by the shrike against the sand. The tail keeps wriggling conspicuously after detachment, which distracts the shrike for a split second even though he has done this several times before. From within his dark mask, he looks up to see the night lizard escape into the blackbrush.

The shrike looks back at the striped tail, still twitching in his hold. It would contain a small amount of fat, which he and his mate could consume in the night. He starts to fly back to the nest, about fifty yards east, carrying the lizard tail in his talons folded against his chest. It was not a meal in itself, but his mate probably had a couple grasshoppers or other insects as she frequently did. The evening crickets in the shadowed areas are already chirping, but there is enough time to reach the nest and his mate before nightfall.

The night lizard also returns to her mate, about twenty yards away on a flat rock. Her climbing is not much affected by the missing counterweight of the tail, as lizards know how to compensate for balance. The tail will grow back after a while.

17

Sunset

"Remember how Dad used to sit out here during sunsets like this?" asked Alma.

"He liked the evening air. That first breath of coolness wafting down from the mountains," replied Lee. They each glanced toward a horizon, with changing skies and mountains in almost every direction, and they were conscious of the breeze against the skin, and the effortless breathing of their clear lungs.

Ned added, "And the beauty of the sunrise and sunset here. Those are almost the only things he liked about the desert."

Lee replied, "But he saw how much all three of us liked it."

There was a pause while they recalled their late father sitting at this very spot in the evening, next to the pavilion at the Palmhaven, with his clip-on sunglasses and a pack of Lucky Strikes, reclining in a steel outdoor chair that could rock a little.

Ned cleared his throat. "Well, it seems like a good time for a budget meeting."

"Still in the black?" asked Lee with a smile.

Alma and Ned smiled in return. "You know it," said Ned. "With the travelers and traffic over the last couple of years, we've built up quite a surplus."

"Enough surplus to build you a real garage?" asked Alma.

"These cars and trucks are getting bigger every year, but you're still working in the old blacksmith's shop," said Lee.

"Well, that's a good idea," said Ned to Lee. "But what about that art school in San Francisco that still mails you brochures? We could afford to send you there."

"Ned, that's sweet," said Lee. "There was a time when I very much wanted that. But now, whenever I leave the desert, I feel uneasy and nervous, and can't wait to get back."

"The desert is what you like to paint, too," mentioned Alma. "That might not be what they want to see in San Francisco."

"Well, here's another idea," said Ned. "Why don't we build a restaurant right over there? You two could run it."

Lee and Alma exchanged a glance, and Ned could see that they were of like mind. "We both like to cook sometimes, but we wouldn't want to do it all day, every day," said Lee.

"We could hire other cooks and waitresses," suggested Ned.

"We can all think about that, and how it might work, but we both voted for a new garage," said Alma with a smile.

"Ned doesn't like being outvoted, even if it's for his own benefit," jibed Lee.

He chuckled. "Definitely could use a new garage. I thought we might do something for you two first."

"Let's make your new garage first-rate," said Alma.

"Room for two medium-sized trucks, and those greasy trenches like we saw in Banning," said Lee.

"Service pits," smiled Ned. "Great for crankcase service and the undercarriage."

"Yes, that!" said Alma.

"E Pluribus Unanimous!" declared Lee, quoting what their late father would say when a meeting reached consensus, though sometimes there were dissenting voices.

Having transformed from caterpillar through cocoon to adult in a few weeks, the white-lined sphinx moth hovers like a hummingbird and sips from a dune primrose. The white petals are still young, and have not grown to their full length and bell shape. But the flower produces nectar. The moth's long proboscis allows her to drink from almost any flower, including bell and tubular shapes.

When the primrose's petals are still small and less obtrusive, a nectar-drinking moth most likely won't brush its fuzzy head or antennae against them to inadvertently gather pollen. That will wait for a future visit. For this moth and flower, and almost all others, pollination is an accidental side-effect. It is not a specific intention as it is for the yucca moth, a uniquely willful species.

The yucca and sphinx moths are chiefly nocturnal pollinators, like most moths, preferring white flowers, which are more visible in the moonlight and starlight than the colorful flowers that appeal to daytime pollinators. In this desert, the Joshuas and yuccas, dune primrose, sand blazing star, and datura are among the night-blooming white flowers pollinated by moths.

Over the generations, the sphinx moth has learned to wake and sip nectar at sunset before its main predator, the bat, emerges at dusk. When the sun is sinking in the high desert, there are many canyons and valleys in shadow, which resembles moonlight enough for the sphinx moth to feel comfortable visiting flowers. If a sphinx moth is hungry enough, it will wake a little earlier and visit a few colorful day-blooming flowers, but that is usually not necessary. They thrive on the nectar of the white flowers, whose blooms are prominent in twilight and luminescent in moonlight.

18

The Street

"Are you sure this is the place?" asked Jem from the passenger's seat.

"The address is right. And it's one of the only buildings with a second floor, like the Captain said," replied Stan. They were parked on a back street in Indio, looking at an unpainted wooden building with a flight of stairs on its left side.

"No signs or displays," remarked Jem.

"Definitely looks shady."

"It's probably illegal, or semi-illegal."

"Well, we only have a half-ounce of gold to sell," said Stan. "We can't get in too much trouble for that."

"I'm okay with trying it. We can bail if it seems too sketchy," replied Jem.

They stepped out of the car and crossed the unpaved street, which was narrow and only a couple blocks long. There were no other vehicles or pedestrians on this Friday afternoon.

"Nice little town, but quiet," said Stan.

"Must be siesta time," remarked Jem.

"That's what a lot of these desert people do in the afternoons, especially in the summer," replied Stan, carrying the gold in a red bandanna tied with a boot lace. As they stepped up to the boardwalk, he shifted the gold from his right to left hand, and the bandanna fell open, scattering the gold flakes and tiny nuggets in the sand below. "Damn!" said Stan.

"Was that all of it?" asked Jem. He dropped to his knees and picked out a couple of the larger nuggets from the grit and refuse, just a few inches away from an expectorated tobacco chaw. Stan joined him, and took out his pocket knife. He used its spoon attachment to begin sifting through the sand, peering at each spoonful for gold.

"Sorry, Jem, my mistake. I hope we can get most of it," said Stan. He spread the bandanna on top of the boardwalk, and they began recovering individual flakes and shining specks from the sand. They saw that it would be a tedious process.

"You're a little uncoordinated sometimes, aren't you?" replied Jem with impatience. "This is going to take us forever, and we won't get it all."

"We'll get most of it. Calm yourself down," replied Stan. "You make mistakes sometimes too."

Then they heard a clattering noise from the corner, and looked over their shoulders to see a small man with a large backpack, stepping with some deliberation in their direction. "Afternoon, gents," said the stranger. He stopped, took off his brimmed hat, and shook it off. He looked to be about 40, balding, with a large mustache and a friendly expression. "Splendid day."

Stan nodded, Jem said hello, and they turned back to their gold recovery, their heads inches from the ground. The man stopped and took off his backpack, watching their efforts with a little smile on his face.

"Excuse my interruption, but how 'bout a pan?" he asked, holding a frying pan. They looked at him blankly, distracted. "You fellas never panned for gold?" he chuckled. "It'll be a lot faster than the needle-in-the-haystack method." He crouched down between Stan and Jem. "Put a handful of sand in this pan, by the side."

"Okay, I'll try it." Jem scooped a handful and let it fall into the pan.

The man unscrewed his canteen and poured a little water onto the sand. "Now I'll gently shake and slightly tilt the pan, like this, and the gold will stay anchored at the top of the pan all by its lonesome, while the sand slides with the water to the lower side. There's other ways to do it, but this is the best for beginners." He shook the pan while minding its tilt, letting more sand and grit slide down with the water.

"A grain of gold is about fourteen times heavier than the same-sized grain of sand," he told them. "Now you take this pan," he said to Jem, "And you can use my gravy pan," he said to Stan, handing him a smaller pan.

"Well, this should go a little better, thanks," said Jem with a wry smile. They each scooped a handful of sand, poured a little water, and started panning.

"Never thought I'd be panning for gold in a gutter," said Stan.

"Well, it's not exactly a gutter," replied Jem. He said to Izzy regarding Stan, "He's a city boy."

"You seem like very capable young men, but my guess is that neither of you are from California," said the man.

"That's exactly right," said Stan, glancing up at the man.

"How'd you know?" asked Jem.

"In California, all the school kids learn how to pan gold," he said. "That's how we became a state."

"Well, I'm glad a Californian came down this street," said Stan.

"One with pans," added Jem. "Thanks."

"I guess maybe you fellas are involved in a mine around here somewhere?" asked the man. "Judging by your nugget bindle, dusty clothes, and scuffed boots. I recognize my own kind." He chuckled.

"We work a couple places north of here, in the high desert," replied Stan. "You know anything about this business here? Good spot to sell gold?"

"Oh yes, they'll pay more than the official channels." He looked at Jem's pan. "Shake it easy, keep the pan more flat. A forty-five degree angle will dump all that glitters."

They each poured water from their own canteens, and kept on shaking and sifting, sometimes swirling. It took time, but they could see it would be far more successful than hunting for glints in the sand. After a few minutes of panning, it looked like they had recovered almost all the gold. "This pan's just sand," said Stan. "We got it all."

"Now if you fellas want to have some better paydays than this, I know of some promising claims that are looking for people to take them over."

"We can talk a little more when we get through with our business upstairs. You say you've sold minerals here?"

"Yep, they'll buy your gold, and within a fortnight it'll be on a ship to Europe or the Orient, where it's worth more."

"Do you have business with them today?"

"No, just passing by. Stabled my horse in the barn around the corner."

"We appreciate your help, mister. My name's Stan, and this

is Jem."

"Call me Izzy. Good to meet you fellas."

"Been around these parts for a while?" asked Jem.

"More than ten years now," replied Izzy. "I'm what you might call a miners' agent, helping out with information and know-how."

"Well, thanks for letting us use your pans," said Stan.

"*De nada.* I'm going to take a break right here, rearrange my pack a little."

"We'll see you in a few minutes, then," said Jem. He and Stan began climbing the wooden stairs up the side of the building to a small landing and door on the second floor.

In the cactus patch at the end of the street, the territorial announcement of the cactus wren cuts across the clearing, beginning at a deliberate speed, then growing faster and louder in staccato iterations until it slows and halts. The wren's warning call was sometimes compared to a clumsily cranked Victrola or a jalopy trying to start, cranking and grinding and then stopping. When he ceases the call, the cactus wren looks around in a challenging way, seeing if his declaration has raised hackles or ruffled feathers. His mate is quietly nesting in a nearby cholla, sitting on five tiny eggs, each less than an inch long.

The wren couple has been at this cholla patch for several seasons, and they are year-round residents. They know the shady pocket on the north face of the mountain where scrub pine needles cover grubs in the spring. They know the current topology of the anthills on the valley floor where they might eat a few ants a day in moderation. They know where every seed will fall in its time, and they know the faces of the other local animals and their dispositions. The wrens become slightly more accustomed to humans they see regularly, especially if the humans behave in calm and unthreatening ways, but they still voice a warning.

The cactus wrens are most comfortable on a cactus, preferably a cholla with its barbed thorns that protect like barbed wire. Predators like the snake and coyote have trouble penetrating the *nopalera* without perforation. When the wrens aren't on a cactus, they get jumpy and frenetic, unprotected and nervous, wary and head-tilting while looking for insects, lizards, or seeds to eat. In the safety and comfort of the cactus patch, they build multiple nests, some of them oriented horizontally with side entrances. Together they construct a concealed nest for the eggs, and a higher one with sight lines for the sentinel roost and decoy. The wrens' mottle and markings become camouflage in cholla. They are perfectly adapted to hot and thorny places. The desert is home.

"Well, they gave us about ten percent more than Sacramento does," said Stan to Jem as they came down the stairs.

"Then there's the five percent that we lost in the sand, if their scale was right."

"I figured that in. Might be worth coming here sometimes."

"Up to the Captain, I guess," replied Jem.

"Are you talking about Joe Haberman?" asked Izzy from the boardwalk.

"You know him?" asked Stan.

"Sure, I've known Joe for years. Met him in the hospital after the war."

"Were you injured in combat too?" asked Jem.

"Can't salute with one arm, and won't salute with the other.

Got a groove on the side of my head, and metal in my shoulder. But the mustard gas that scarred my lungs is what drove me to the desert. You must be the young fellas working the Anaconda with Joe."

"That's us. We're headed up there now. Probably stop by Cottonwood Spring." said Stan.

"Didn't bring enough water for panning, eh?" Izzy inquired with a smile. Stan and Jem chuckled, and Izzy continued, "Would you fellas be willing to give me a ride up to Twentynine? I'm supposed to meet a man there tomorrow. My horse is in the stable for the weekend; he trotted through some cholla, got needles under his shoes."

"Sure, we can give you a ride. We were planning on stopping at the Anaconda though. Do you get along with the Captain?"

"Oh, we've had our ups and downs over the years, but we get along fine. Haven't seen Joe in a while, would be good to talk to him."

"Well, climb on in," said Stan.

Izzy loaded his pack in the backseat of the Studebaker, then sat next to it. Stan started the car, and after turning on a couple of dusty streets, they were quickly north of Indio, traveling towards Cottonwood Spring.

When humans weren't present, many animals visited the spring, shaded by fan palms in clumps of three or four, interspersed with cottonwoods, some creosote rings, and a couple black willows bending their branches over the water. A round-tailed squirrel drank at the same time as a thrasher, then came two squash-blossom bees, and some gnats. After a few seconds or a minute, each of these left satisfied, and others took their places.

A black-throated sparrow sipped, a mourning dove couple visited, then came a Gambel's quail followed by his mate. A cottontailed rabbit drank next. The rabbit was the slowest drinker, taking more than two minutes to sip only a little water. He had angled himself so that he could see the trail that brought humans and other land-based predators down the hill to the oasis. When he heard humans approaching, and then saw and smelled them, he bounded to the shade of a young green creosote, thick with yellow blossoms and buzzing bees, in the other direction beyond the fan palms.

The humans spent a few minutes at the spring, then went back up the trail. The cottontail rested in the shade and listened to the bees.

After filling their canteens at Cottonwood, they turned up Utah Trail towards the Anaconda Mine and tent cabin.

"Some good claims around here for sale or lease, if you guys are interested. Onyx, copper, vermiculite," said Izzy.

"Vermiculite?" asked Jem. "What do people use that for?

"Insulation, fireproofing, grow plants in it. Many things."

"Copper prices have sunk. Not much manufacturing going on," said Stan.

"That's true, but they'll rise again," said Izzy. "Next time we get in a war."

"Thanks for mentioning the claims, Izzy, but I seem to be busy enough with the gold mining work I'm doing now," said Stan.

"Yeah, the Captain keeps us busy, and the pay is okay," said Jem.

Izzy cleared his throat, almost as loud as a cactus wren's warning. "You guys know that he's not really a Captain?"

"Sure, he told us that," said Stan. "But he's the Captain of our mining crew, so that's what we call him."

"Well, if he's your Captain, he's the strangest you'll find. You work for him, you respect his authority, so you probably get along fine. He likes a rank-and-file situation."

"He's treated us okay. And he knows mining."

"He has his theories about mining, but they haven't necessarily panned out," said Izzy towards the front seat, where Stan and Jem were watching the road. He paused for a few seconds and then went on. "There are a lot of people that Ol' Joe doesn't get along with. He respects rank like he was still in the Navy. Out here, it's more unstructured and . . ." He hesitated and came up with the word, ". . . democratic." He paused further, as if waiting a reaction, then continued. "Haberman sees it like climbing a mountain, with people higher and lower, but nobody gets treated like they're equal."

"Well, he's taking us on as equal partners for our new venture," said Jem.

"New venture? A new mining company? Maybe struck gold?" asked Izzy.

"Something like that, but we really shouldn't talk about it yet," said Stan.

"Okay then," said Izzy. "I'll keep quiet."

After a couple minutes of silence, Izzy spoke again. "I remember the first time I met Joe Haberman, in a ward at the Veterans' Hospital. An orderly and a nurse came around three times a day to each bed, about two dozen of us, and they put a couple drops of morphine under each tongue in the room. That was about all they did for eleven days, which I counted, before the surgeons got around to us."

The car was silent for a few seconds. "Thanks for your

service, Izzy," said Stan. "How are you feeling these days?"

"Well, some of my body parts are past their prime, but all the cogs in my noggin still rotate."

"Izzy, there's usually a decent meal at the campfire on Friday nights," said Jem. "Maybe you can join us if it's okay with the Captain."

"That would suit me fine," replied Izzy. "Good way to spend the evening after a week of hard work. I got my own fork."

In a few more minutes, they were at the Anaconda. They parked the Studebaker in the rock corral, and started walking uphill towards the mine and the cabin.

"They were hitching horses and mules in this corral just a few years ago," said Izzy. "Times have changed."

"I'll take a good truck any day," said Jem. "Of course, Stan's fancy car is all right too," he added.

"This sedan might work a little better if you were taking a young lady on a date," said Stan.

"Well, that might be true in some places, but farm girls appreciate a good truck," replied Jem.

"Not too many farm girls around here, and only a few town girls."

"Well, we know a couple of nice ones," replied Jem. "We should be dating them."

"Maybe so! But we'd have to ask 'em, and their opinions count too, more than ours," said Stan.

"You fellas probably don't even realize that this is one of the best times of your lives," said Izzy. "Oh, to be young again."

As they stepped over the ridge in the waning daylight, they saw the Captain and William Quine standing by the side of the fire ring at the cabin, eating from coffee mugs and looking in their direction, not recognizing the third man. "'Lo there!"

called the Captain.

Stan, Jem, and Izzy climbed up to the plateau, and walked by the shaft to the campfire. "Hello, Captain," said Stan. "We ran into an old friend of yours."

Haberman peered at Izzy. "More of an acquaintance. Hello, Izzy," he said without enthusiasm.

"Good evening, Joe!" replied Izzy. "Been a while, good to see you again."

"Has Izzy been trying to offload his two-bit claims?" asked Haberman of Stan and Jem.

"Not really," said Stan. "He mentioned vermiculite and copper, but we told him we prefer gold."

"Izzy likes to tell stories, but he doesn't do any real mining. Just talks about it," said Haberman.

"Now, Joe, there are different jobs for different people," said Izzy. "I'm a miners' agent."

"You're a prospector, Izzy. You tell fishy stories to hard-working people for good money."

Izzy snorted and raised his eyebrows. "Good money? Never seen any good money, don't even have a car. Ask my horse."

Haberman chuckled. "I don't mean to be giving you such a hard time, Izzy. After all these years."

"The sun shines and the rain falls on both of us just the same, Joe, and we get our disability checks on the same day each month too."

Haberman laughed. "You got that right. I'll tell you what, Izzy, why don't you stay for some dinner. We got rabbit stew with taters, carrots, and onions."

"Smells mighty good, too. Thanks, Joe, I'll be happy to join you fellas for dinner. Where'd you get the vegetables? You're serving what rabbits eat along with the rabbit."

"The taters came from Ry Keane's garden, the carrots and onions from Twentynine Palms."

"You know, ever since that second grocery opened up in Twentynine, they've both done better business," said Izzy. "Farmers come from a long way out to bring them produce."

"It's a growing town," replied Haberman.

"How's Ry been? Haven't seen him in a while."

"Doing well, I think."

Izzy took out a kerchief and wiped his brow with his good arm. "Last time I saw him, he was raising a little posse to run off that guy who tried to stake a claim and build a wall around that one big oak tree."

"I remember that. Not sure what happened, but that crew has been gone for a while," replied Haberman.

"Good to hear. Ry's wife and the teacher lady can take the school kids for lunch under the oak again."

"That's a nice spot," replied Haberman. "Only full-sized oak for a hundred miles or more."

"They were talking about making it a public park, protecting it for everybody to use," said Izzy.

"Good idea. Ry said that somebody tries to claim it every couple of years."

While the others were talking near the campfire, Stan and William met inside the cabin. Stan took a package out of his bag. "These are fresh ones. Two pounds of the best Coachella Valley medjool dates."

"Thanks, Stan," replied William, exchanging a bread tin for the dates. He continued, "This is a good batch of cakes. Have a great time at the party, wish I could make it."

"I wish you could too. I don't think that Jem has guessed

anything yet."

"He hasn't said anything to me about it. I think you've kept it secret."

"Hey, did you bring any mesquite cakes that we can eat now?"

William laughed. "Hungry, eh? Sure, I bake six dozen at a time. Pass these around." He handed a paper bag full of mesquite cakes to Stan, who thanked him and walked out the door to the campfire, where the Captain, Jem, and Izzy were still talking and watching the last rays of sunset.

19

Dusk

Quine placed the dates on the cabin table. Then he stepped outside, but in the other direction from the campfire and around some boulders, into the dusk. A grasshopper hopped ahead of him, then leapt into a clump of grass and chirped. As the last rays of the sun faded, one star and then another twinkled into view, and then more as the sky merged into a darker blue. Then the stars became brightly vivid, and the Milky Way spread from horizon to horizon and beyond. He paused on a flat rock, and glanced at the familiar stars that, to him, formed a small *olla* pouring into a larger one.

Then he remembered what his Chemehuevi grandfather had told him on such a night a couple decades earlier, when he was an eight-year-old boy. They were walking together after a good meal in the early evening, and Grandfather had stopped to consider the sky.

"Stars beyond stars . . . does that school let you look at the sky, William?" Grandfather paused and took a deep breath, seeming to Quine like he wanted to inhale the scene into his lungs and bloodstream. He exhaled and smiled at young

Quine, who was shaking his head yes while looking upwards. Grandfather continued, "You know, William, when I was your age, my own grandfather told me something. He told me lots of things, but there's one I remember very well tonight, and I will tell you just as he told me. He said to me, young one, you know that you have one father and one mother, but two grandfathers and two grandmothers. Those four each had two parents, so the next generation doubles to eight great-grandparents, then the next to sixteen and then thirty-two." He paused and looked at Quine. "If you go back many years, and then many more years, for we have been here a long time, we have thousands of ancestors, more than we can count. Just like those stars in the sky tonight." He beamed at young Quine, who looked at the stars and imagined them as relatives.

Then Grandfather, too, surveyed the constellations, and saw a wild array whose light was partly tangled in the branches of the unruly mesquites, thorny acacias, and flailing Joshuas. Then he glanced down at his grandson, who was looking up at the stars and illuminated by them, his eyes dark pools of bright reflection. "And you know what else, William? Our grandfathers' grandfathers, and the grandmothers, all our relations, all our ancestors, when they have reached the end of their days, they are said to have 'passed on.' But somewhere they are watching us. They want us to do well, and they want us to be happy people. They wish that we could learn from their mistakes, and our own mistakes, and they're glad when it seems like maybe we do learn a little something."

Young Quine asked, "Are they the stars, looking at us?"

Grandfather paused to gather his words, and then replied. "Our people are watching us like the stars, and they are many like the stars, but they are not the stars . . . they are something else, we know not what. They might be like the sun sparks and *mortero* chaff floating between the stars, imagine that! But whatever they are, we respect and honor them. It is our way."

Then they were silent for a long moment, to restore a kind of equilibrium after many words. They looked at the constellations in their familiar patterns, arrangements known for centuries yet still evolving in their own time. The individual stars were twinkling and pulsing with a dynamic of change and distance, which to Grandfather and young Quine expressed a wholeness and majesty that shimmered within their sensibilities.

On the other side of a juniper a few feet away, a pair of white-crowned sparrows in their nest stopped listening and went back to sleep. They had wakened slightly at the footsteps and voices, but slipped back into slumber when it was quiet for more than a few seconds. Their nest was sheltered from the west wind, and not easily approachable from below. Then Grandfather spoke again. The sparrows woke and listened.

"Let's go back," said Grandfather. They stepped away. It grew quiet to the sparrows, and they barely heard the crickets chirping in the starlight.

20

Hark!

William returned to the campfire, still thinking of the stargazing with his grandfather from decades past. The others had put their stew mugs aside and were eating mesquite cakes.

"Do you fellas always eat this well on Friday nights?" asked Izzy, as William sat down between Jem and Izzy, cross-legged on the ground.

The Captain laughed. "This is better than usual. But William's mesquite cakes are the topper."

"I'll say!" said Izzy. "It's like taking the taste buds on a tour of California. Walnuts from up north, dates grown in the palm deserts, mesquite and chia from around here. Then comes a hint of exotic lands, the cargo of bananas and cinnamon from afar."

"Thanks," said William. "I like how these ingredients work together." The others nodded in agreement, and kept eating.

"It's a good night for a feast," said Haberman after a moment. "We're celebrating a special occasion. Our strong young colleague here, Mister Jem Parker, turns 21 on Sunday."

Everyone congratulated Jem, shaking his hand or slapping his back.

"Doing anything special for your birthday, young man?" asked Izzy.

"Well, Stan has a surprise planned. But he hinted that women are involved, so I have a good guess."

"I hope you have yourself a drink or maybe several, disregarding constraints of unjust prohibition," said Izzy.

"Oh, I've done my share of drinking in the past," said Jem, "and I don't really need it."

"Turning 21 is sure different than in my day," said the Captain. "Won't be able to belly up to a bar legally."

"Jem will probably have a fine time whether he drinks or not," said Stan.

"No doubt!" replied Jem with a smile.

Izzy cleared his throat. "Now, Joe, I know you don't like alcohol in your camp. But seeing that it's a weekend and a special occasion, maybe this bottle of quality shine can pass around the circle?" As he spoke, he reached into his bag and pulled out a clear bottle with a cloudy liquid. "Some of Indio's finest."

The Captain glowered at Izzy. "Why'd you bring that here?"

"It's the weekend, Joe, and the bottle was in my pack. Relax yourself a little, like the doctors told us both."

Haberman glanced at the faces around the circle, lit by the dancing light of the fire, and said, "Well, every man can decide for himself whether he wants to drink or not. But remember that you fellas were going to do some work on that claim beyond Stubbe Spring tomorrow."

"You've come a long way, Joe, letting the enlistees think for themselves," said Izzy. "Here, why don't you take the first drink." He passed it to Joe, who took a look at the bottle and then passed it on to Stan, who also studied the liquid.

"I'll take one sip just to taste it. I drank some in Chicago, but haven't been too interested out here in the desert." Stan uncorked the bottle and lifted it to his lips. After tasting, his eyebrows lifted and he smiled a little. "That's got a bite to it. The bootleg liquor in Chicago was smooth, but this has character."

"Well, you're kind of a character yourself," said Jem to Stan as he passed him the bottle. They smiled. Jem took a swig and said, "That's not bad." He put the cork in the bottle and handed it to William, who immediately passed it back to Izzy.

Izzy uncorked it and took an enthusiastic gulp, then recorked the bottle and spoke. "I see you've got your pipe filled, Joe. I'm going to smoke the other half of this stogie if you don't mind." He reached into his pocket and removed a cigar butt, which he extended toward the camp fire and lit.

"Now, Izzy," said the Captain, "this might be a good time to hear one of your stories. Like how tin miners will get rich because everyone in the world will be eating three meals a day out of tin cans under tin roofs."

"Not sure if I've heard that one, Joe," said Izzy. "Sounds like a tall tale." He took a drag from his cigar.

"Or maybe you can re-tell the one about how vermiculite will soon be in every household, insulation and mattress stuffing and plant-growing."

Izzy exhaled, then replied. "Sure, I can tell a story, but maybe you can share one of yours first, Joe. Tell about how Captain Joe Haberman sailed the seven seas and mined the twenty-three deserts of the world, yet somehow he's still just as broke as ol' Izzy."

Haberman chuckled. "You're making me laugh now, Izzy. I can't be too mad at you when you've got me laughing."

"Does anybody want another refreshing drink from this bottle?" asked Izzy. The miners said no thanks, or shook their heads, and he tightened the cork and put the bottle in his pack.

"Well, since my audience is fairly sober, I guess I can tell a story," said Haberman.

"Glad to hear it," said Stan. William and Jem smiled in anticipation.

Haberman put his pipe aside, cleared his throat, and spoke. "This tale occurred a few years ago, when there was still some good placer mining to be done in the area. You fellas have been mining ore from deep in the ground, which is a different process altogether. It used to be more feasible to find gold, grains and flakes and even nuggets, on hillsides and dry stream beds, where it had washed down a mountainside from a lode higher up. People could pan it, if they had water, or use a machine called a dry washer if they didn't. That's what I used to get the samples that you two sold in Indio."

"Now one time there was this greenhorn who came to the desert from some coast, maybe a city on a bay or somewhere like that. A prospector was talking to him about various claims available for sale and transfer, and the greenhorn was interested. He thought a 'prospect' was a place with potential mineral deposits, and that's true, but to the prospector himself, the greenhorn was the prospect, because he could be reaped of cash in exchange for the location and rights to a claim that sometimes wasn't much of anything."

"So the prospector took Mr. Greenhorn to a sunny hillside on a pleasant afternoon, and they started panning for gold on the alluvial plain, using water from their canteens and water bags. It wasn't long before they found several grains and a tiny nugget. The coastal fella had the glint of gold in his eyes, and he wanted to get started right away. He forked over some bucks to the prospector, who had the transfer papers on hand. A couple signatures on the dotted lines, and the deal was done."

"The prospector shook his hand, wished him luck, and moved on. The greenhorn worked for the rest of the day. He carefully noted the exact locations where specks of gold were found, and drew a diagram in pencil on a paper bag. This fella maybe knew a little more about mining than he let on. He knew that the typical pattern of placer gold was fan-shaped, with the gold spreading down the hillside from its source higher up, potentially a rich lode. By diagramming the samples on the ground and then up the hill, the range of dots on the map would narrow to a point that was near the source."

Haberman continued. "When he had a dozen dots on his map, this gentleman noticed something peculiar. The shape of the fan was opposite of what it should have been. The point of the fan was near where he was standing on the *playa*, and the arc of the fan was across the hillside in front of him. Then he noticed that there was a bit of something that looked like gunpowder on the tiny nugget. From this information, he figured that the gold had been loaded in a shotgun with some pebbles, and fired into the hillside from the plain below. There was no rich lode up the hill."

"The coastal gentleman rode back into town, and the next morning he contacted the sheriff. He showed him the diagram and the telltale nugget, and the sheriff said 'aha' when he read the prospector's name on the deed. They picked up the notorious prospector, and made him refund the money to the gentleman. He didn't get arrested or anything like that; he just rode off into the sunset. But I can't speak for the dark cloud of his conscience."

Izzy had a little smile on his face. "That's a good story, Joe. Entertaining and imaginative."

"That one seemed kind of educational," said Jem.

"Yeah, a cautionary tale," remarked Stan.

"My story was good because it's true. Now I'd like to hear one of Izzy's. He knows how to ladle from the steaming crock." Most of the group smiled or laughed, then Haberman continued. "All prospectors are storytellers, of course, but Izzy is the most silver-tongued of 'em all."

As the Captain spoke, William was putting another log on the fire, and Jem reached into one of his bib overall pockets for chewing tobacco. As he opened the pouch, he realized it was the wrong package. "Oops, this isn't tobacky, it's carbide for the lamp." The group laughed, and he exchanged it for the other pouch.

"Why, thank ya for the compliment, Joe," said Izzy. "I'll be glad to tell you a story, and it's one that I've never told anyone. I think this is exactly the right audience," he said, looking around the campfire at Stan, Jem, William, and Joe.

"It was some years ago," Izzy said. "I was a spry young fellow. I climbed to this strange place high in the mountains, very hard to reach, up one sheer-sided peak and then another, the only route up as far as I could tell. I figured out that climb myself, never told anyone, and now can never go there again. I'm not going to tell you exactly where it is, but I'll describe it to you. It might be a mile away, or it might be a hundred miles away. But it's in the wild Mojave, and it's the wildest place that I've seen in this desert or anywhere else."

"I camped overnight in the foothills, then was up before

dawn to begin the ascent. In the months before, I had tried a couple other approaches but they fizzled out. This idea looked like it might work, but I knew it wouldn't be easy. This peak is in a range that tends to be bypassed, not known to be rich with minerals, and I never heard of anyone scaling it to the top. But I was an excellent climber in those days, good upper body strength, strong wrists and arms, and I only had to pull up 125 pounds because that's how little I weighed." He made a muscle with his bicep. "I don't weigh much more than that now, and I'm still strong for my size and age, but I'm not going up that mountain again."

"Anyway, a month before, I had seen a potential route when I scaled up a ways to reconnoiter. It looked rough all the way up, but one part was real tricky. About halfway up the peak, the ascent became impossible and impassable. Sheer vertical with overhangs. But there was one ledge that could be used as a runway to jump across a chasm to another peak, which had some potential handholds most of the way up from there. It looked possible if I could make a long jump of 15 feet. That's a long way to jump, but I read that the world record was about 24 feet, so I knew that a 15-foot jump was possible. I'm not a long-legged guy, but I was a good athlete in those days. I went home and practiced for a month, running several strides and then hurling myself into the air. I trained like it was the Olympics, eating healthy food and refraining from smoking or drinking. For the first week, I could only do twelve feet, but I stretched, practiced, and modified my approach, and eventually I could jump about 16 feet on my best days."

"So this day was it. I felt well-rested and ready. The sky was clear, with very little wind. You miners are lucky, you don't have to worry about prevailing winds when you're down in the ground like a mole. But up on the mountain, I was checking the wind and clouds as I went. Even though it was calm, it still took me about three hours to climb up to the crossing point for the first time. I looked it over, and used a branch to sweep the loose pebbles and sand off the ledge. I also swept some fragments of bighorn spirals, points and cracked arcs, from when the big bucks had strutted across that ledge to crash horns. The ledge was not as long as I estimated, so my approach would be a little shorter than the optimal length, but I had practiced some variation. I looked down into the chasm, and it would be a drop of a thousand feet onto rocks if I didn't make it. But my landing area on the other side looked inviting. It was a sandy notch with a little shade from some pinyon pines."

"Now you might ask why I would take all this effort to climb this particular mountain, even knowing of my interests in geology, geography, and mineralogy. I had traveled near this mountain in the past, and studied it from more than one angle. It was sheer on all sides, but you saw a different skyline of peaks from each side. There was no tall summit at the center of the mountain. I had climbed a nearby hill and studied the mountain with a spyglass. It looked to me like a crown of peaks with a large empty space in the middle. Maybe the open space was a crater, or maybe it was a sweet hidden valley that no one had ever seen. What if I could climb there, and explore it? Maybe there was gold, and maybe it was worth blasting a tunnel through the side of the mountain to bring out the ore. But that's a lot of maybes, and I get ahead of myself."

"First I needed to leap over the chasm to the climbable peak. I would have to leave my backpack on this side. I sat it down behind a large round rock, and took only a small flask of water in my front pocket, along with the spyglass. Then I stretched, took a stance at the end of the runway, ran, and leapt! And I made it. Did a somersault in the soft sand and ended up in the cool shade. I took a short break there, as it would be the only shade for the rest of the climb."

"Then I made my way up the peak, from handhold to handhold with only a few good footholds. After an hour of difficult climbing, I came to a place where I could see between a gap in the rocks. It wasn't wide enough for me to climb through, but I could see into the valley. And that what it was. Taking out my spyglass, I could see its length and breadth. It was about five miles long by three miles wide, and most of it was thick with Joshua trees. They were healthy-looking, and blooming on a spring day like today, but like a lot of the ones you see at the highest altitudes of their range, these trees weren't very tall, only about twelve feet at most. But they were thick and healthy, with many branches and flowers."

"After I noticed the Joshua trees, I started to see some very unusual things. In the near part of the valley, there was a pair of giant sloths. You heard me right: giant sloths. They're extinct everywhere else, but they still exist in this valley. They were massive and strong, bigger than oxen. When they stood up on their hind feet, they were taller than the Joshua trees. Close to fifteen feet tall, I reckon. Their long snouts were eating Joshua blossoms from the top of the trees, and they most likely had propagated the seeds in their scat throughout the valley. I watched them for a little while. They were slow-moving, not peppy at all. You might even call them slothful. But they were very strong, with powerful sloping shoulders, and large claws like bears."

"When they stood up, their backs straightened, and their

shoulders were square when they reached. But most of the time, they had all four feet on the ground, their shoulders were sloping downwards, and their spines were bent forward in a way that looked stressful. They slouched like old brokedown miners." Izzy glanced in Haberman's direction. "I started to think that bad posture was one of the factors that caused the giant sloths to become nearly extinct. You young fellas should sit up straight," he gestured at Jem, who was slouching at the other side of the campfire. Jem chuckled and rearranged his posture in an exaggerated way for a moment, then sat straight.

"But that wasn't the strangest thing I saw that day. At the far end of the valley was a round lake, about two miles in diameter. I thought maybe it was a crater fed by underground springs. It was surrounded by white quartz sand and Joshua trees, and the water was a beautiful deep blue. Like everything else in the valley, it seemed to be pristine and untouched by human hands. I assumed it was a freshwater lake, but then I saw some things that made me think it was saltwater. The lake had some ripples and waves going back and forth. It wasn't a windy day, so it seemed like something was agitating the water. Then I saw something small, pointed, and white breach the surface. Maybe a shark's fin? No, not a shark. It was the corner of a fluke, and then the entire tail emerged and slapped the water, causing more ripples and waves against the shore. Then a plume of water sprayed from the blow hole, and there emerged a huge, white -"

Faster than they would have thought possible, Haberman was upon him. He lifted Izzy off the ground and glared him in the eye. "Out! Be gone with you, Izzy!" Then he carried him for a few feet away from the campfire, in the direction of the road, and let him drop to the ground. Izzy grabbed his pack and disappeared into the darkness without another word.

Stan and Jem were nonplussed. William stood up. "I was going to Twentynine tonight anyway. I can give him a ride. Goodnight, fellas." He grabbed the package of dates from the cabin, then walked down the hill after Izzy.

21

The Nut

At noon on Saturday, the short workday was almost finished. Laden with ore-filled backpacks, the three miners hiked a winding path downhill with heavy steps and a moderate pace. Picks, hammers, and shovels were strapped to the sun-faded, canvas packs, but each miner could still appreciate the altitude's characteristic greenery of pinyons, junipers, jojobas, and bright, new-leafing mesquite.

"Think that's enough sample to keep this claim another year?" asked Jem.

"The value of the labor counts too. That's us, gents," said Stan with a smile.

"I like coming up here," said William. "Wonder how much gold is in the ore."

"Cap said it was getting a little better as the adit went deeper," said Jem.

"The Pinto claim has been the best lately," said Stan, turning his head to speak over his shoulder to the others.

"Eyes on the trail, bud," said Jem in a jocular tone as Stan almost tripped on a protruding root. "We should be working

Pinto then," continued Jem. "Anaconda's shot."

William said, "This claim here is hard to reach. The mountain is better without a road."

"I wouldn't be surprised to see us all working at Pinto before long," said Stan.

"How's the approach?" asked Jem.

"You can get a truck to the bottom of the mountainside, and up the wash a little ways. Then it's a few steps between some boulders up a side wash," said Stan.

"Do you have to cross that huge basin?" asked Jem.

"No. I'm not sure if this peak is considered part of the Pinto range or not. It's definitely on the way there. It's called Libélula Peak."

"Libélula?" asked William.

"Yes," said Stan. "That's Spanish, right?"

"It's like saying 'level' or 'balanced.' It can also refer to dragonflies," replied William.

"Hmmm. . .I don't remember seeing any dragonflies there," said Stan. "But maybe it's been too dry."

They slowly made their way downhill, alternating their glances between the rocky path at their feet and the surrounding vista of Joshua trees, scrub oaks, pines, junipers, yucca, nolina, and wildflowers. Jojobas and manzanitas dotted the hillside, with their leaves vertical to minimize the effects of the midday sun, oriented to face the gentler rays at the beginning and end of the day. It was the first day of the spring season to reach eighty degrees Fahrenheit on this mountainside, warm and dry, but still comfortable in the shade.

"This is a good place for pinyon pine nuts. I'll have to come back here in the fall," said William.

"Do you use the pine cones that have fallen, or pick them off the trees?" asked Jem.

"A little of both. The best time is just before the cones open, before the birds and squirrels get the nuts."

"Do you have to crack each cone?"

"If you warm the cones over a fire, in a pan or net, they open. Then you can shake out the nuts, and roast 'em. I'm going to try for more this fall so that I can trade for medjool dates in Coachella Valley."

"Looks like there's much more rainfall here than Coachella or Twentynine," remarked Jem.

"People talk about how the high and low deserts have different plants and wildlife, but this seems like a third type of desert," said Stan.

"Higher altitude. More rain. More green plants, and pines," agreed Jem.

William was silent for a moment, thinking of the Serrano side of his family. They had descriptive names for each level of the mountains and valleys, but he couldn't remember those names. He recalled that the term for this level included the color green, but he had only heard those words a couple times. At altitudes of about 3500 feet and above, evergreen pinyon pines and junipers grew alongside the evergreen Joshua trees and yuccas. In the spring and summer, they were joined by the vibrant green of mesquite and acacia.

"It's almost summer at Twentynine, and it seems like spring at this altitude," said Stan.

"But it's still winter up on Gorgonio," said Jem, gesturing toward the snow-capped peak. From much of the Morongo Basin, you could see either Mount San Gorgonio or Mount San Jacinto, the tallest mountains in southern California at about 11,000 feet above sea level. But this was one of a few places where you could see both mountaintops at once, without nearer peaks intervening.

As they rounded the corner of a rock outcropping, they startled a pair of grazing mule deer, who ran a few lengths uphill. As the deer reached the top of the ridge and saw that their escape was assured, they paused to look over their shoulders at the humans, infrequently seen at this altitude. After a few seconds where each species stared at the other, the mule deer ambled over the ridge.

"You don't see too many deer down below," said William. "They like to nibble on the green leaves up here."

"They look different from the white-tailed deer back where I come from. These have long black tails, and longer ears," said Stan.

"You know, it's the same difference between cottontail rabbits and jackrabbits," said Jem. "The jacks have longer ears and black tails."

"That seems like an interesting coincidence of nature," said Stan, and they continued winding downhill. They reached a point where they could see the truck parked below, at the edge of the flat that was stark with hard-packed sand and scattered foliage, a contrast to the lush hillside.

Soon they were nearing the bottom of the hill, and the path began to level. They came to a place where the trail weaved between a large boulder and a desert lily thick with blossoms. William saw Stan and then Jem accelerate as they went through the gap, and flail their hands aroound their head and shoulders. "Bees!" shouted Stan, as he took off his cloth hat and swatted at a few. As they ran and lurched down the path, their heavy backpacks caught up with their forward momentum, knocking them both to the ground, where they fell laughing and still waving hands at a couple persistent bees. Jem slipped his arms from the backpack straps, grabbed the short-handled pick, and half-swung it towards the bees.

As William stepped through the gap, he saw bees swarming and buzzing around the flowering bush. There were a few bees sitting on the rock to his left. He looked one in the eye and nodded, then kept walking down the path towards his young co-workers.

Still sitting on the ground, Stan and Jem looked at him. "William!" said Jem. "Why did the bees leave you alone?"

William took off his pack and sat it on the sand, positioning the shovel on top. Then he sat down. "I have a treaty with the bee nation," he said with a little smile on his face, aware that it might sound odd. In some native languages, the word for "species" and "nation" was the same.

Stan and Jem looked at each other, and then at William, not entirely sure if he was joking. "How does that work?" asked Stan.

"Well, part of it is body language. And, uh, projected intention. I don't set myself in opposition to them." They looked at him blankly. William continued, "Animals always look at each other's facial expressions and physical attitudes. When they see me as relaxed and maybe even a little friendly, I don't seem so much like an enemy or predator."

Stan and Jem remained silent, still catching their breath, and William wasn't sure if his ideas were reaching them. He continued. "Sometimes I let the bees land on my shirt and drink a little sweat. They like the minerals."

"Well, that's a different way of looking at things," said Stan.

Looking at William's face and mulling over his words, Jem spoke haltingly, replaying images in his mind. "Yeah. Like those mule deer we saw up there. They looked at us and the expressions on our faces. When they saw that we weren't hunting or chasing them, they stopped running and did some people watching."

William and Stan smiled. "I think you got that right, buddy," said Stan to Jem.

"They're not enemies, they're neighbors," said William, using a slightly jovial tone to express a viewpoint that he knew might be foreign to the others, but had always seemed natural to him, and implicit.

"Well, I've never been stung by a neighbor," said Jem. "But I've never been stung by a bee either, so I guess you're right."

They stood up and positioned their backpacks and tools, then walked the short distance to the truck, where they took off the packs again and emptied the ore into the truck bed, a little more than half-full. The tools and the empty backpacks were then locked in the steel box.

"Are you guys hungry?" asked Stan.

William nodded yes, and Jem said, "You bet."

"I heard some people talking about the roadhouse over by Warren's Well," said Stan. "Apparently they have a barbecue pit, and offer a good menu on the weekends."

"I'm up for it," said Jem. "How about you, William?"

"Sure," William replied. The three of them got in the cab of the truck, and started traveling north and west towards Warren's Well.

22

The Fountain

The miners' truck slowed as it approached the highway, and then stopped. A herd of cattle was plodding across the road and then veering west in a cloud of their own dust. Several Herefords looked at them blankly with white faces, their reddish hides glazed with sand, tails swinging and swatting, ears twitching. Two of the cows stopped in the road to relieve themselves on the hard-packed sand.

A pair of cowboys on horseback rode up to the edge of the herd, and pointedly ignored the truck. Even with the bandannas pulled over their mouths and noses to filter out dust, they were talking loudly and laughing.

"This might take a while," said Stan.

Jem said, "Ry Keane mentioned these guys."

"I heard about 'em too," said William. "A local in Twentynine said they took wire cutters to his fence and drank from the *tinaja*."

"They trample over everything, Ry was saying," said Jem. "The guy who owns the cattle company is related to the sheriff, so they get away with a lot. They go from one water source to another, cutting across other people's property. Open range laws. The ranchers in Texas are more polite."

"Not much green grass to chew on recently, with the drought," said Stan.

"These cows look skinny and parched," observed William.

After some minutes, the cattle moved on, and the miners continued to the roadhouse, which was within sight of Warren's Well, a public water source. A few cars and trucks were parked near the well, and people were filling containers. A slow-spinning windmill and some adobe buildings stood north of the well, with clusters of healthy mesquite in tree, shrub, and sprout form. There were many mature, thick-trunked Joshua trees, some still in bloom. In the foreground was a row of rectangular troughs and oval stock tanks with water piped a few feet downhill from a tank connected to the well and its pump.

They found a place to park at the roadhouse, where the graded lot was less than half-full with trucks, automobiles, and a few horses tied to horizontal wooden rails. "This place will probably be packed tonight," said Jem. They glanced at the ore that half-filled the truck bed, which looked like plain rock and probably didn't contain much gold.

"Nobody's gonna bother that," declared Stan. "We can check on it every now and then."

They pushed open the swinging doors and stepped into the high-ceilinged room. At the far wall, there was a bar with some scattered drinkers, and a food table to the left of the bar. On the right were five round tables populated by locals, working people, travelers, and cowboys. In the middle of the room, four long tables could seat about eight on each side, but these tables were mostly empty on this mid-afternoon.

A few beams of sunlight penetrated the grimy windows high on the western wall, illuminating slow-rising plumes of smoke and floating dust. Loud conversations reverberated through the half-empty room, with glassware clinking and bottles thumping on the wooden tables, occasional laughter, and the ring of two cash registers.

A few patrons glanced up at the young miners, and they walked over to look at the food table. There was a tray with some chipped beef in a white gravy, and a plate that offered slices of toasted white bread. William recognized this combination from the Navy, where it had a colorful nickname. Next was a platter of barbecued chicken wings that looked a little dry. Another platter was stacked with boiled potatoes, one with sauerkraut, and then a deep pan with mashed sweet potatoes embedded with miniature marshmallows, topped with molasses.

There was a small fan with clean brass blades at the end of the table. Battery powered, it streamed a current of air above the food to repel flies and gnats. The fan also rustled the curtain and a four-foot strip of yellow flypaper coiled high in the corner of the room, which looked somewhat clean, and from a distance resembled a festive streamer.

A bartender said to them, "Have yourself a seat, fellas, and one of the gals will come around to get your drink orders. The weekend spread only costs two bits."

They glanced at each other and smiled a little. "Is it worth the money, you think?" asked Stan of Jem and William. They took seats at the empty end of one of the long tables, and a brunette, middle-aged waitress was there almost immediately.

"Good afternoon, gentlemen," she said. "What are we drinking?"

"I'd like a cup of coffee, black," said Stan.

"Iced tea for me," said Jem.

"Sarsaparilla, thanks," said William.

"Comin' right up," replied the waitress. "Are y'all passing through the area?"

"Been here a while," said Jem. "We've been mining over by Twentynine."

"Striking it rich, I'm sure," joked the waitress. "You fellas look too clean to be miners."

"We're more dusty during the week. Saturday's one of the cleaner days," said Stan.

"Well, relax and enjoy yourselves," said the waitress. "Even with the revenuers always nosing around, folks end up having a good time here."

"Thanks. We'd like to try your food, too."

"Two bits a plate, free second helping. The weak survive, and the strong thrive. Dishes are up there," replied the waitress.

They each filled a plate with items from the food table, and sat back down to eat. After a few bites, they all looked up at each other.

"They went heavy with the salt on everything," observed Jem.

"So people will drink their beverages more," replied Stan.

"Seems like the kind of place where locals can get alcohol on the sly," suggested Jem.

William put down his chicken wing. "I think our meal last night at the cabin was better."

"Heck yeah," said Jem. "Rabbit stew and mesquite cakes were a feast. But this is still better than those canned sausages that Stan eats every day."

They chuckled. Stan said, "I'm getting a little tired of those. Trying to phase 'em out."

As the waitress brought the drinks to the table, there was a sound of thundering hooves, first distant, then louder. Some of the roadhouse customers looked at each other with expressions of annoyance and disgust.

"Here they come again," said the brunette-wigged waitress. "The cowboys who think they own the world and all its water."

As she plunked each of their drinks on the table, the miners noticed that the waitress had tattoos of three ravens flying down the length of her arm, with the final raven's beak open at the thumb and forefinger. It looked as if the ravens were delivering the beverages.

"Do the ravens ever say 'nevermore?'" asked Stan.

"They say it every time they have to slap some guy for getting too fresh," replied the waitress. "Nothing personal, honey," she said with a smile as she turned around and walked away from the table, which erupted in laughter when she was a few yards away.

"She told you what's what," said Jem, chuckling in Stan's direction.

William said, "She made it sound like all three ravens do some slapping."

"It's a conspiracy of ravens!" exclaimed Stan, his face red with laughter and slight embarrassment. They all chuckled some more, and tried to stop laughing to sip their beverages.

A few miles away at the ore mill, Joe Haberman was trying to negotiate with Ryland Keane.

"Now Joe, you know I can't extend credit here," said Ry. "No matter how long you've been around. Nine out of ten miners go broke, and the tenth just barely gets by. Some of them have wealthy backers from L.A. and places like that."

"I don't need credit really. Just advance me a truckload of that banged-up timber so we can build supports. And maybe some straight rails and another ore cart." The Captain leaned forward as he spoke, and didn't notice that his pipe had extinguished.

"Can't do it, Joe. Gold mining isn't a credit business, it's a gamble."

"Blazes! Ry, you've seen how much better the ore has been lately. The new mine has a sparkle."

Ry cleared his throat and decided on a tactful approach. "Well, this business is based on optimism, Joe. Glad you've got that. And hard work too. You have a good crew."

"Thanks. This is the best damn crew I've ever had, and maybe the most promising claim, too. You know I always do cash 'n' carry with no debt, but this is different. Trust me, old friend, you'll see."

Ry paused to consider. He looked at the sky, which was sunny and clear, then at the concentration table, which was half-full, and then at the windmill a short distance away, turning listlessly clockwise. He thought about the junior miners working with Haberman, three likeable fellows trying to get a start in life during a time of economic collapse. Then he looked at Haberman.

"Tell you what, Joe. I'll front you a half-load of lumber so you can make things safe for your crew. After you pay me for that, we can talk about rails and carts."

"That's a deal, Ry. World of thanks. You won't regret it," said Joe.

"You want mostly support stulls, overhead beams, or wall slats?"

"Some of each, but mostly the round stulls and square beams, just a few slats for now."

"All right. I have more stulls and beams than slats, good lumber just sitting in the shed. You might as well use it."

Joe started to reply, but Ry stopped him. "No need to thank me again, Joe. I'll help you load the wood."

The roadhouse doors popped open, and five cowboys entered loudly, waving and yelling to one of the round tables, "They're all yours, boys." At the table, another group of five cowboys stood up, greeted the newcomers with equal bluster, and moseyed towards the door.

Rather than taking the departing cowboys' table, cluttered with used mugs and full ashtrays, the five new arrivals moved towards the nearest of the long tables, which was empty except for the three miners.

The tallest of the cowboys, who seemed like the trail boss, nodded to William, Stan, and Jem, and said to his crew, "I'll go for a little something to get us started." He went to the bar and began talking to a bartender.

The other cowboys, two younger and two older, sat down and looked over the food on the miners' plates. "How is it, fellas?" said one of the older men, reaching into a pouch of tobacco.

"A little dry and salty, but not bad," reported Stan.

The younger cowboys ogled the food and leaned over the table. "Those chicken wings look real good," said one. "Can I try one of yours?" he asked William.

"Okay, here's one," said William. "But you might want to get your own."

"Maybe I will, maybe I won't," said the young cowboy, who the miners now recognized from the road. The two older cowboys were starting to nod off in their seats, one of them with a chaw in his cheek.

"Can you pass the pepper, William?" asked Jem.

"William?" smirked the other young cowboy. "We got another Willie Boy here?" The others at the table looked at the young man in surprise for a moment, at his overconfident expression and weak blond mustache. All were taken aback by his reference to the 1909 manhunt.

"Why do you call him 'Willie Boy?'" asked William, looking the cowboy in the eye. "He was 27, same age as me. Not a boy."

Stan added, "That Willie Boy episode was more than twenty years ago. Our friend William had nothing to do with that."

"These two are injun-lovers and traitors to their race," sneered the other cowboy, pointing at Stan and Jem across the table, who stood, their bench sliding on sand and sawdust. William stood too, shoulders squared towards the cowpokes.

"You're awfully runty to be mouthing off," said Jem to the cowboys. They saw that he was barrel chested and strong, Stan was tall and long-armed, and William was fit and athletic. Jem continued, "Listen cowboy, William is one of us, and if you want to start something, all three of us are on it."

The standoff was interrupted by the trail boss, who returned carrying a tray of eight small glasses with a cloudy, colorless liquid. "Here's a round of mint sodas for the table." He sat down the tray but remained standing. "Now what's going on here?" he asked.

"We were just talkin'," mumbled one of the younger cowboys.

"Frakes and Scroggin, drink this shot, then go out and tend to the horses before you eat. Brush out the cockleburs and the goatheads and the cholla buds from the manes and tails," said the tall cowboy. The younger cowboys chugged their "mint sodas," sat the glasses back on the table, and took on sullen expressions as they filed out through the swinging doors.

The conversations in the bar resumed, quietly at first, and the miners realized that everyone had been listening and watching them during the tense moments. "It's peppermint schnapps," said Jem to Stan in a low voice as they were sitting back down at the table.

"Those two sometimes get a little mouthy," said the trail boss by way of apology. "Have yourselves some soda with a kick," he offered with a little smile.

"Thanks, don't mind if I do," replied Jem. Stan and William smiled and nodded thanks, and then each drank a shot glass of schnapps.

"What were those two fools saying this time?" asked the trail boss.

"They had some problem with my Native ancestry," replied William.

"I'm going to give those guys another talking to," replied the tall cowboy. "By the way, my name's J.P. Robusto." He shook hands with William, Stan, and Jem, as they introduced themselves.

Robusto drank his shot, and sat down the glass. "You know, I heard that before you Natives showed the pioneers the mountain passes in this desert, they had to take boats down to Panama and cross the isthmus on mules, back before the canal was built. Or go around the horn."

"The Serrano and Chemehuevi know these transverse ranges well," said William. "That's part of my heritage."

"Pleased to meet you, William. The Natives weren't hostile or violent when they first came into contact with the Europeans," observed Robusto. "They were friendly and helpful, like with

Pocahantas."

"And Sacajawea," mentioned William.

"But then when the newcomers wanted more land, they started wars while saying that the Injuns were warlike," said Robusto. "I have some Native blood in me, not enough to call myself an Indian or anything like that."

"Well, even though it's only a small part of your ancestry, you took an interest in the subject, and it's given you a certain perspective," commented William.

The waitress brought a cup of coffee for J. P. Robusto, and refilled Stan's cup. "I figured that you miners would get along with J. P.," she said, smiling. "He gets along with everybody. He wasn't raised a cowboy."

"You guys are miners, eh? How's that going?"

"Well, we're not getting rich," said Stan.

Jem shook his head in agreement. "We're just getting by. Most of the gold was taken out decades back."

Robusto sipped from his cup, still hot. "It has to be better than running cattle. Not much grazing grass left in this desert, can't fatten 'em up."

"One good thing about mining ore, drought doesn't affect it so much, not like it does farming and ranching," said Jem.

"The drought's been on for three years now, and we have tension with settlers everywhere we go. No water holes to ourselves these days."

"This area seems to be growing, even with the heat, the drought, and the depression," observed Stan.

"I'm thinking about changing jobs," said Robusto. "Maybe throw in with a mining outfit. In the summer, it'll be nice and cool below the surface."

"How long you been driving cattle?" asked Jem.

"A couple years. I had to drop out of college when the economy crashed."

"A college cowboy, eh?" said Stan with a smile. "I spent some time in college back east."

"If you're looking for a mining job," said Jem, "You might check the bulletin board at the American Legion in Twentynine Palms."

"Thanks," said Robusto. "I might do that real soon."

"How far back is your Native ancestry?" asked William.

"Goes back quite a ways. On my mother's side. Ojibwe and Potawatomie from Illinois and Wisconsin, before they were states."

William smiled. "You're the third Potawatomie that I've met. The other two were nice fellows too."

"I'm real glad to run into somebody who wants to talk about this. You know, there were about 150 years when the Natives around the Great Lakes got along fine with the Europeans, who were mostly French looking for pelts and furs. From about 1650 to 1800."

"The Natives probably helped them out too," said William.

"Oh yes," replied Robusto. "They showed the Europeans the three water routes that connect Lake Michigan to the Mississippi River, so they could trade and travel all the way down to the Gulf of Mexico if they wanted."

"Three routes?" said Stan. "I lived in Chicago for most of my life, and I only know of one."

"Well, you should have talked to some more Natives," said J. P. with a smile.

"I met some Potawatomies at a pow wow right after I got out of the Navy," said William.

"I really haven't known too many," said Robusto. "What were

they like?"

William smiled. "We had a good time. They invited me to join their drum circle, since I was the only Serrano/Chemehuevi there. It was in New Mexico."

"Some good food there? Green chile?" asked Jem.

"Sure," said William. "We had some venison sandwiches that were delicious. Better than the food at some places," he said, glancing around. The others chuckled a little, and William continued. "These guys brought a birch canoe to the pow wow. For their people, it was the main transportation for many generations before they were relocated to the reservation in Oklahoma."

"The Potawatomi had a trail of tears, like the Cherokee and a few others," said Robusto. He looked at Stan and Jem and explained, "Forced march."

"That was inhuman," said William. "My Native ancestors didn't have to move as far, but they had to move."

"Did you guys take that canoe out on the water?" asked Robusto.

"Yes!" said William, laughing. "They had to put it in water every few hours so that it wouldn't dry out. The birch bark would start to curl and stretch as it dried, and it might pop a seam. So we left the pow wow and drove around at night in this unfamiliar part of New Mexico, looking for a creek or pond, any water. Eventually we came to a little town that had a circular fountain in the center of town. Nobody was around, so we took the canoe down from the top of the car, and put it in the fountain. Then all three of us got in the canoe, and we paddled around the fountain, singing a Potawatomi song that they knew."

"Was there maybe a little fire water involved?" asked

Robusto.

"Well, it sure wasn't minty soda!" replied William with a smile as most of the table chuckled. "Anyway, we were paddling and singing in the birch canoe, having a jolly time, when suddenly two policemen pulled up. But they were both laughing, couldn't keep a straight face. We explained the situation, and they said that it made sense. We tied the canoe to the top of the car, and went back to the pow wow."

The miners and cowboys at the table were smiling, picturing the canoe going around the town fountain with vocal accompaniment. "That's a good story," said J.P. Robusto. He took out his tobacco pouch and started rolling a cigarette.

"You know what, guys?" said Stan. "Probably about time to be moving on. Big day tomorrow. It's been good meeting you, J. P." Jem and William nodded in J. P.'s direction, and spoke their farewells.

"Glad to meet you fellows," replied Robusto. "Maybe I'll see you again sometime."

The two older cowboys, who had been asleep for most of the conversation, mumbled goodbye to the miners. They stood up and headed for the door, leaving money on the table for the bill and a tip. Their waitress saw them from across the room, and she waved and smiled.

As the miners got in the truck, Jem called "Bye now!" to the two younger cowboys, who were bent over a horse's posterior, removing cockleburs from the tail using a comb, and sometimes scissors that were attached to a pocketknife. They glanced up and then ignored him. The miners turned east on the road, and were soon on the way to Twentynine Palms.

"You know," said William, "I might be related to that other

William, the long-distance runner. Carlota too."

"I'd like to hear more about that situation," said Stan. "You've been in a talkative mood today," he said to William.

Jem was driving, and peering intently through the blowing dust and sand. Some of the mountains in the distance were barely visible.

"Well, I'm getting to know you guys better," replied William. "I thought of something I'd like to run by you two."

"I'm listening," said Jem, and Stan nodded.

William started to say something, but the truck hit a bump, and the clatter of rocks and tools in the truck bed was louder than his words. He spoke again.

"You guys ever hear of using cyanide on the tailings?" he asked.

"I overheard some talk," said Stan. "It can yield small amounts of gold, but uses a good amount of cyanide."

"The Captain was talking about doing it," said William. "Sometimes he has to dip into his pension to pay our salaries. We need higher yield."

"So where does the cyanide go?" asked Stan. "It's a deadly poison, and it can last a long time."

"It wouldn't be too hard to find a place where no one ever goes, and dispose of it there," said Jem, hesitantly. "It's a big desert."

"But what if it drips down into the groundwater, poisons an aquifer?" asked William.

"Even if it's on the rocky surface, it might dry into a powder. Then the strong winds could stir it up, and people might breathe it in," said Stan.

"You know, I really don't like it either," said Jem. "My people are all farmers, and we never had the best land, but we always kept the land in good shape for the next generation."

Some moments passed while they all thought it over. "This brings up another question," said William.

"Go ahead," said Stan and Jem, almost simultaneously.

"You know how the Captain says that we'll split the ownership of the new mine, and each of us will have an equal say?"

"Yeah. That seems to be really important to him," replied Stan.

"But what if we all vote one way, and he votes the other way?"

"Three to one should be a winning tally," said Jem.

"But would the Captain accept the vote," asked William, "Or would he see it as a mutiny?"

"Hmmm. Good question," replied Stan, and Jem slowed the truck as a cloud of dust obscured the road.

$$23$$

The Cabin Table

Later that Saturday afternoon, Stan drove to a public well near the Oasis of Mara, where he filled a pair of five-gallon buckets, several jute bags, and a couple of canteens. When he returned to the Anaconda cabin, Jem was the only one remaining, but he was sleeping in a hammock suspended between an exterior corner of the cabin and a pole that the Captain had anchored in concrete. It was a warm afternoon for April, sunny and near eighty degrees at this altitude, but as always, cooler in the shade. There had been strong winds from the west, intermittently up to thirty mph, but the gusts had calmed and become pleasant zephyrs.

On the other side of the cabin, Stan placed the washtub in a clearing between boulders, a suitable distance from cacti and acacia thorns. Then he went into the cabin, poured from a water bag into the kettle, and hung it on the crosspiece in the stone fireplace. He inserted a page from an old newspaper under the dry branches, then lit the paper with a match. As the fire ignited and the kettle began to warm, he went outside and poured the bulk of the container water into the galvanized tub. It was not enough to fill it even half way, but would be workable for a bath.

When the kettle was almost boiling, he took it to the tub, where it would raise the temperature enough to be more comfortable, though not hot or even warm. He took off his boots and clothes, then lowered himself into the bath, watching the water level rise with his displacement. "Just like Archimedes," he said to himself, then picked up the bar of Lever soap and made lather to shampoo his hair.

After he rinsed his hair, he soaked in the tub, enjoying the shadows and stillness of the late afternoon. Water is always on the mind here, he thought to himself. Everyone carries a canteen, jug, or water bag, and is always thinking of where they will fill it next, on the way to or fro or around. In Chicago, on the shore of a great lake, with plumbing and faucets and fountains everywhere, water was taken for granted.

What would he be doing in Chicago on a Saturday night like tonight? Any number of things; maybe seeing a film at the small neighborhood theater, or sitting in a clandestine beer garden watching some guitarists play, maybe walking on the beach, going on a date, or maybe going to the chess club and playing a few games in that cellar filled with cigar smoke. He mostly had enjoyed living in a big city, with multiple universities, many different neighborhoods, and people from all over the world who worked in every possible occupation. It presented opportunities and involvements.

But tonight? Maybe he would read a little by lamp light, and go to sleep early. The mind would be uncluttered, and he would sleep well in the clear, quiet air. He appreciated the clarity of the desert more every day, it seemed.

A few minutes later, the tub contained the accumulated dust

and sweat of a week's mining, which he dumped near a jojoba bush that looked dry, like almost everything. There were three bags of fresh water remaining, and he stood up and rinsed, first himself and then the tub. He left a couple bags of fresh water for Jem, and put a half-bag of water aside to wash the windshield and hood of the Studebaker in the morning. Then he grabbed the clean towel and dried himself, and put on some of the clean clothes he had laid out nearby.

Carrying his canteen with the strap over his shoulder, and clutching his towel and soap awkwardly under his elbow against his side while he held the dusty mining clothes in front of him, he went back into the tent cabin and dropped his dusty clothes to the floor, and laid the clean items on the table. Then he lathered his face and shaved in the tiny mirror on the wall next to the window. He found a pair of scissors to trim the edges of his fast-growing sideburns and then over the ears. He was thinking of the town girls, Lee and Alma, and he wanted to look presentable at the birthday party the next day. He knew that Jem would be preparing in similar ways later that day or in the morning.

The lingering daylight of Saturday faded as they recovered from the work week. Reclining in his cot near the window, Stan tried to study the text and formulae in a small handbook of static mechanics, but soon he set it aside and dozed.

When he woke, it was dark, and Jem was snoring in his cot on the other side of the room. He walked outside and looked at the almost-full moon rising above the rocky hills, and listened to some coyotes in the distance, howling and yipping. How many were in the pack? Probably not as many as they made it sound. He felt a cool, fresh breeze on his arms and face, and thought to himself, yeah, I could get used to this. Then he went back to his cot and slept.

A few hours after sunrise on Sunday, Jem sat at the cabin table with a newspaper, studying the box scores and drinking thick coffee. It had been a quiet birthday so far. Sparrows sang outside the window, then stopped. He heard Stan's car returning.

"Happy Birthday, Mister 21-year-old!" said Stan as he swung open the cabin door. Like Jem, he was dressed in his best casual shirt that hadn't been involved with mining.

"Thanks!" said Jem with a smile. "Looking forward to the surprise."

"Are you ready to go?" asked Stan. He walked over to the cabin table and picked up the container of mesquite cakes.

"I ate a couple of those cakes. Shouldn't I bring something to the party? I don't want to show up empty-handed," said Jem.

"It's your birthday! You just bring your newly mature self, and we'll take care of the rest."

"Well, okay then," smiled Jem. "My guess is that we're driving north?"

"You're one hundred percent correct. Adults are smart," said Stan. Jem chuckled. They walked outside to the Studebaker with its newly clean windshield, got into the car, and the motor started easily. Stan wheeled it around and past some yuccas and cacti, and they were soon on Utah Trail northbound to Twentynine Palms, then east to Palmhaven Cabins.

In a few minutes, they turned into Palmhaven and parked. Ned was looking under a car's hood at the service station, but he glanced up, recognized the Studebaker, and waved. Then they looked to the east and saw the pavilion under the palms, decorated with streamers and homemade banners that said

"Happy Happy Birthday, Jem!" and "21 At Last!" Lee and Alma were sitting at a picnic table, smiling in their direction. The cabins, the office, and the house seemed quiet, and the palm trees swayed only slightly in the breeze. Jem and Stan got out of the car and started walking towards the pavilion.

"Wow," said Jem. "This is going to be a great birthday. Thanks for setting it up, Stan."

"Good food and good company under some palms on a beautiful day. Nothing better."

"One thing," said Jem. "Do you think this is a double date, or just a birthday party with friends?"

"It seems to me that it's a birthday party with our good neighbors and friends," replied Stan.

"It seems to me that it could develop into something more," said Jem with a smile.

"Well, what we might want isn't necessarily what they want. We'll see. Just enjoy yourself like any 21-year-old gentleman about town."

"Ha," replied Jem. "You're not so ancient, Mister 23-year-old wise man."

"I'm just kidding around, joshing you."

"You're not that much wiser than me. A wise guy, but not wiser," said Jem in a jesting tone.

Stan chuckled and said, "You might be right about that," as they approached the pavilion and the sisters, who seemed aglow even in the shade.

As Jem had closed the car door and stepped across the sand, a cholla segment was clinging to the heel of his polished boot. It was dislodged by a narrow ridge of bedrock. The rounded, inconspicuous bud had hooked on his heel while they were leaving the Anaconda cabin a few minutes earlier. Transported and released, the cholla bud sat on the desert sand, where it might sprout roots if nourished by a rainfall in the next several days. Or it would be more likely taken by the wind or a passing animal to a place near or far. It might grow into a branching, multi-segmented cholla cactus six feet tall or more, with spikes like toothpicks in all directions, and each spike studded with microscopic barbs angled against removal. To the punctured victim, the spikes will seem at least as vexatious as the quills of a porcupine, or the spikes of a puffer fish.

Those who know the desert respect the personal space of the cholla, but they still might become inadvertently involved in its reproductive strategies, as Jem did when he stepped on the cholla segment, carried it on his boot in the car, and then propagated the bud as a potential clone several miles away from its origin.

Cholla most frequently reproduce by snagging in this manner that is promiscuously asexual, clinging to agents of the animal kingdom who are mobile but sometimes lack a specific awareness. The lightweight, spiky buds attach to almost anything that moves. They also reproduce sexually via pollinated flowers, but sometimes years go by without enough rain for the cholla to produce blossoms.

A cholla near the Anaconda had been struck by lightning on the night before Haberman arrived, and the clouds released only a few drops of rain as they passed overhead. Split and stressed by the lightning, the cholla dropped a pile of segments over the next weeks, many of which were carried away by the wind. By stepping and transporting one of these windward buds, Jem became its unwitting agent of propagation and eventual reproduction.

"Happy Birthday, Jem!" said Lee, and then Alma, who held up a round cake with white frosting, decorated with Jem's name and age in golden icing.

"Thanks! That looks like a great cake," said Jem.

"Alma made it," said Lee. "She's the best baker in the house."

"I think it looks better than it tastes," said Alma. "Both of us are better cooks than bakers."

"Hope you like it," added Lee. "But the other food we made will be better."

Alma sat the cake on the table and started to slice it. "We're not using candles during these dry times."

"Good idea," said Stan.

"Twenty-one candles might be a fire hazard," said Jem.

"You've reached a dangerous age," said Stan, and they all smiled. Alma handed Jem a plateful of cake, and then gave one to Stan. She cut a small slice for Lee, and then one for herself.

"We've decided that cooks are more like artists, and bakers are more like scientists. We're both artists," said Alma.

"Stan, you're a man of science," said Lee. "You'd probably be a better baker."

"How do you figure that scientists are better bakers?" asked Stan.

"Well, with baking, you have to be precise with your measurements, especially with yeast and baking soda and so forth," said Lee.

"It's like a science experiment. Sometimes the experiment fails and everything explodes," joked Alma.

Lee laughed with Stan and Jem. "We haven't had one of those in a while," she said.

"So then why are cooks more like artists?" asked Jem between bites.

In the pause while Lee and Alma were still eating cake, Stan asked, "And how did you two get so good at both?"

"Cooks are more in the moment," said Alma. "We add a little more of this, a little less of that, knowing what ingredients are best that day, or just having a feeling about what's right. Like an artist."

"I sometimes get into the same frame of mind when I cook as when I paint," said Lee. Jem and Stan were still eating cake, while the sisters had taken a couple of bites and put down their plates.

"Is this coconut?" asked Stan.

"Yes, it is," said Alma. "But if it were a really good cake, you wouldn't have to ask." She looked at her sister, and they both laughed. Stan and Jem chuckled with mouths full of cake.

After he swallowed the bite of cake, Jem remarked, "Eating coconuts under palm trees . . . are you sure we're not on a desert island?"

They smiled. "These palms don't grow coconuts, silly," said Alma in a tone of mock-seriousness.

"They grow dark-colored fruits that are like berries, but they're more seed than fruit," said Lee. She pointed at the palm trees on the other side of Cabin Five, she added, "There are a couple clusters way up top behind some fronds, you can barely see them from here." They looked over at the palm fronds against the blue sky.

"Too dry for many palm fruits this year," said Alma. "Even with the same water table that supplies our well."

They were all silent for a moment, eating cake, glancing at each other a little more, smiling, then looking away shyly. Stan and Jem noticed that the cabins seemed quiet, with some cars parked around the perimeter but few signs of habitation.

Finishing a bite of cake, Stan asked, "Not too many guests in the cabins tonight?"

After a moment, Lee replied, "All eight are occupied. But they don't make much noise on Sundays."

"Four of them are long-term, month to month. Pensioners and retirees," added Alma.

"And a sheriff's deputy too," said Lee. "We don't have much trouble when his car is parked right there."

Jem said, "Ned looks like he's busy at the station."

"We invited him to join us, and he might drop by," said Lee.

"He was real interested when we told him there would be two kinds of cake," said Alma, smiling. Jem smiled with her, noticing her dimples.

Lee said, "He was asking about those mesquite cakes."

"I brought a couple dozen," said Stan. "I invited William too, but on Sundays, he spends time with his relatives and bakes these cakes." He opened the box of mesquite cakes, which sat beside him on the bench.

"He bakes six dozen every week, and gives them all away, or trades them for ingredients to make more," said Jem.

"These are always delicious. Better than our cakes," said Lee, reaching for one of the small cakes.

"We have some enchiladas coming, but it won't spoil our dinner to eat one of these," said Alma when Jem passed her one.

"Or two," said Stan, already reaching for a second small cake. In the morning hours, he had felt a soreness in middle of his back from yesterday's work, but the soreness had disappeared as he sat in the palm-shaded pavilion, sharing food and drink with people whose company he enjoyed.

"The enchiladas are probably ready," said Lee, standing up,

and then strolling towards the house.

"Oh, they'll be delicious too," said Alma.

Jem picked up the pitcher of iced tea and refilled their glasses. "You two sure throw a swell party," he said to Alma with a smile, which she returned.

"Well, we wanted to make sure your first birthday in our little town was a good one," she said.

"This feels like the right place to be," replied Jem. "This town in general, and this spot in particular." And spending time with you, he thought as he looked at Alma, with her skin glowing gently and a pleasant smile.

"Well, look who's here," said Stan, and they saw Ned walking over from the gas station, having scrubbed the grease off his hands and changed into a clean white shirt. He held a white envelope, and passed it to his other hand so that he could shake hands with Jem.

"Happy Birthday, Ol' Jem!" said Ned. "Here's a gift certificate for two dollars worth of gasoline."

"Shucks, that's better than vintage wine," replied Jem. "Thanks, buddy."

"Ned, you're just in time for the enchiladas of course," said Alma, gesturing towards Lee, walking from the kitchen with a covered platter. "Need any help, sis?"

"I've got it covered," punned Lee, setting down the platter with a pot holder and an oven mitt. She removed the cover, and steam arose.

"Ahhh . . ." said everyone at the table.

"You guys are in for a treat," said Ned. "My sisters make the best enchiladas."

"Been looking forward to this meal all week, breaking our backs down in that mine," said Jem.

"I was about ready to eat that cactus right there," said Stan, pointing to a large prickly pear cactus.

Ned, Lee, and Alma looked at each other and then started laughing, which puzzled Stan and Jem.

"Uh…what?" said Stan, smiling a little as if anticipating the punchline of a joke.

"Funny you should mention that, Stan," said Lee. "It's one of the main ingredients in the enchiladas."

"Cactus enchiladas? Have you taken out all the thorns?" asked Stan.

"We usually call 'em spikes, spines, needles, or barbs," smiled Ned. "And remove every single one."

"Why don't you sit down and join us, Ned?" asked Alma.

"I don't want to be a fifth wheel," replied Ned. "You make a couple fine-looking couples," he said, looking at Alma sitting next to Jem on one bench, and Lee next to Stan on the other, with a picnic table full of food and drink between them.

They all smiled and looked away, down, and then briefly at each other, slightly embarrassed to be seen as couples, but pleased.

"Save me a couple enchiladas in the kitchen," said Ned, then added "please," and walked away smiling. He looked back and saw the four of them looking self-conscious for a moment. Then they picked up their forks and started to eat.

24

Cetology

Back at the Anaconda, reclining on his cot and looking at the canvas ceiling, Haberman recalled a conversation from decades earlier, when he was a young enlistee in the U.S. Navy. He had spent much of this particular shore leave at a Long Beach saloon. One night he was drinking at a round table with a few young cronies and some old salts, who were telling tales and sharing their opinions freely. There were multiple conversations at the table and in the bar, but Haberman was leaning against a wall near the table with his pipe in his hand, and his mug on a small shelf nearby. Back when both of his legs were still healthy, he made a principle of standing when elders needed seats. He was listening to an older fellow with a long white mustache who had been in the Confederate Navy during the Civil War, and more recently spent time in the south Pacific.

"What you want to avoid is a whale on the lee-beam," advised the veteran, speaking loudly over the saloon's hubbub. Haberman remembered watching the old man's left boot, hobnailed and scuffed, nudging the spittoon as it swung erratically to the irregular rhythm of his pronouncements. The spittoon, stabilized with a ballast of expectoration, bobbled but remained upright. "The whale might feel hemmed in between your ship and the shore, and react violently," he explained to whoever would listen. "But a whale on the weather side, that can be good. One time we had a whale, larger than our ship, that surfaced on the weather side, and shielded us from strong gales, which might have run us aground. We traveled side-by-side with that giant beast, parallel to the lee shore. Oh yes, it's a beast, but it's a thinking beast. He guided us around the island to a cove that had some protection from the storm."

The old salt noticed young Haberman standing there, listening more intently than most at the table, who were involved in other conversations or just staring into their drinks. He paused his story and looked Haberman in the eye. "Perhaps you'd like to buy an old sailor some refreshment?" Haberman had shaken his head negatively, grabbed his mug, and walked away. His own experiences with briny leviathans were different from this sailor's tales. He didn't like how the old rebel talked about whales, how they could be advantageously used as tools or props, supporting actors to the human drama, and then reaped as sources of oil, meat, and wealth, sacrificed to the demands of human greed.

Whales are always major figures when they appear, reflected Haberman. He mulled over the old sailor's remarks and his own evolving responses, looking back more than two decades later, at age forty-two, looking up at the canvas roof of the tent cabin. He had surmised that whales sometimes act in ways that seem clearly good or bad to human objectives. But he told himself that these great beasts, as a species and particularly as individuals, have their own agenda and willpower that can be hard to figure from our perspective. Haberman had learned to regard the leviathans as a reminder of vast unknown forces that could change a person's life with a sweep of the fluke. But in some unsounded depth of his mind, he knew that this regard was a conditioned reflex, like that of a prey animal after repeated experiences. It was not the comprehensive, tested, queried, and peer-reviewed understanding of a hyper-rational or scientific person. His gut feeling, which eventually became a strong conviction, was that the whales should be respected as sovereign royalty in their maritime domains. But how should a whale be regarded in the desert? His mind still trawled for an answer.

William Quine remembered a time when he and his grandfather were sitting cross-legged in the desert before sunrise. The mountain air was cool and fresh, and they breathed slowly and deeply without thinking of their breath. Rays of the sun were not yet visible, and the moon was also unseen. Thousands of stars shone on the desert landscape in silence.

In the sand between Quine and Grandfather was a cluster of translucent white flowers that held the starlight and reflected it back into the night. Some of the rays reflected onto the two of them. Grandfather had called the flower *"ku'u,"* with two syllables, and they sat with the *ku'u* between them like a campfire. To William, the first syllable of *ku'u* was like the starlight traveling to the white flower, and the second syllable was the same light reflecting off the petals into his eyes, where it might illuminate his mind and heart.

After sitting for a few minutes, Grandfather looked up at the stars and began singing. The song was Chemehuevi, and William didn't know the literal meaning of the words. He felt himself responding first to the rhythm in the syllables, and the consonants that were like drum beats. With each moment, there grew in him an awareness of the ancient strength in the bones of the song, and a consciousness that had endured.

Grandfather held his palms over the blossoms as if they were a fire providing warmth, bringing his hands and fingers together evenly and then moving them apart. He looked and listened towards the stars as he sang.

Later William learned that the European-Americans called this flower "sand blazing star," which seemed like a good name. But he preferred *ku'u*. He would always remember this time with Grandfather and the *ku'u*, but he didn't remember what happened before or after. He wasn't sure if this was a memory or a dream that came from somewhere other than memory. Maybe it was the memory of an earlier dream. Or was it the dream of a childhood memory?

It seemed like a dream that had blurred its connection to memory over time, but his grandfather was real in the dream, as real as a fresh memory from an ordinary day, or even more so. He thought about it again, and looked at the images in his mind. There was some kind of truth in this vision, which he could see dimly but not understand. Now that he had returned to the desert, he wanted to find some *ku'u* to visit by starlight, where it might again reflect and illuminate.

25

A Squeeze of the Hand

At the base of the support posts at each corner of the Palmhaven's pavilion, the fruits of the prickly pear cacti were plump but not yet ripe. At the far end, unnoticed by the birthday party, a mockingbird looked over the green fruits. In the late summer, when they ripened, they would range between purplish-pink and dark burgundy in color. Then the bird would puncture the oval fruit's skin with jabs of her beak between the spikes. The mockingbird relished the sweet pulp that enclosed its tiny seeds.

This particular patch of *nopalera* had sprouted from the seeds dropped by another mockingbird decades earlier. The fruit was one of three elements of the prickly pear traditionally harvested by desert dwellers, but less frequently by travelers, who would bypass most of the desert's spiky things on their way to places where the vegetation had less intimidating defenses. For humans to eat the prickly pears, first the spines were cut, plucked, or burned off. Sometimes they would be removed by rolling the fruits in the sand. Then, after paring the skin and maybe straining out the seeds, the fruits could be enjoyed raw, used as a jelly, or frozen. They could be hand-squeezed, then mashed or otherwise juiced to make *agua fresca*, a nutritious and refreshing drink.

A white, scaly substance clinging to some of the cacti's pads is secreted by a parasitic insect living under the scale. The tiny insect, called cochineal, uses the scale to protect itself from the sun and drying wind. About 20% of the cochineal's body weight is comprised of carminic acid, which is harvested and processed to make a red dye that is more colorfast than others. It is widely used in textiles and food coloring. The curlicued scarlet border on the blouse that Lee wore to the birthday party was made from cochineal in Mexico, where it has been grown commercially for decades, and exported to many countries.

The young green pads of the cactus, called *nopales,* are consumed in several different ways. After cleaning, and boiling or roasting, the pad's needles can be plucked, scraped, or burnt away. The *nopales* can then be cut into strips, battered, and fried or baked to make cactus fries. Or they might be served with eggs and salsa at breakfast, or used in soups and stews. They can be included in a taco, or used as a tasty and nutritious vegetable in various recipes. Both the pads and fruits can be the principal ingredient in jellies and candies.

Shortly after sunrise, Alma had harvested a couple pads from the younger prickly pear in the field behind the main house. When she sliced them after boiling, it seemed to her very similar to slicing a bell pepper. After being baked in the enchiladas, they would have a taste somewhere between okra and green beans, an interesting complement to the black beans, peppers, onions, and *ranchero* sauce.

Surrounded by Joshua trees, William Quine walked through

the valley and looked at Mount San Gorgonio on the horizon. It was forty miles in the distance, but could be seen clearly, snowcapped and shining in the sun. Good afternoon, *Qwirriqaych,* he said to the mountain, using its Serrano name. Its giant sister to the south, *Ayaqaych,* was obscured at this spot by other mountains that were smaller but nearer. He had spent most of his youth in the sun shadow of these mountains, he thought to himself, but was now living in their rain shadow, and was glad to be there.

He strolled towards a hillside a half-mile distant, where he would sit and observe the valley, the mountains, and the sky for the rest of the afternoon. After he sat still for a while, animals would resume their normal activities, and sometimes overlook his presence entirely. He liked observing them not as a hunter or scientist but as another living being, neutrally with no specific intentions, the same way that he watched the clouds moving slowly across the landscape, their shadows darkening one hillside and then another but so rarely erupting in rain.

At the Sherman Institute, which many called "the Indian School," the students had been warned against idleness, and the faculty and coaches worked to prevent it with activities, chores, classes, and drills during most waking hours. But his grandfather had showed him the virtues of stillness and quiet observation. They had sat together on similar hillsides for hours without speaking.

As Quine reached the foothills and gained some elevation, he sat against a flat rock. He took off his boots and socks, and enjoyed the feel of the sand under the soles of his feet, at first slightly cool in the shade, but then grounding and subtly energizing. After he sat for a short while, he again felt like he was part of the desert, connected, maybe not in the same ways that his Native ancestors had been, but grounded on the same ground.

A deluxe 1931 Packard Eight sedan pulled into the Palmhaven Service Station, and honked at the pump. Ned and his employee Ricky were already on their way out the door to the car, which seemed overfull with five loud, well-dressed passengers.

"Fill 'er up with ethyl," declared the driver. Ned nodded, "Yes, sir," and took the nozzle from its holder at the pump. He found the gas cap at the rear of the Packard, and Ricky began washing the windshield.

A mustachioed man in a jaunty hat leaned out the rear window and looked back at Ned. "How far to L.A., bub?" he asked.

"About 140 miles as the raven flies." He didn't feel the need to use the word 'sir' a second time. "But as the car drives, it will take you anywhere from four to twelve hours. Sometimes longer," Ned replied.

The man said, "Gee, thanks," in a sarcastic tone, retracted his head, and started to say something to the other passengers as he rolled up the window. Ned glanced over at the bright pavilion in the late afternoon sun, with its twin clumps of palms, and the couples at the picnic table. Alma and Jem were sitting with their backs to him, about a foot away from each other, and they were holding hands on the seat between them. From what he could see of the angles of Lee and Stan's upper arms, they were doing the same. Ned smiled to himself again, and watched the couples laughing together at the table.

He liked these fellows, Stan and Jem, a few years younger than himself, but interested in some of the same things, like cars and baseball. During the past few weeks of springtime, he saw that his sisters enjoyed their company too. Now he imagined Stan and Jem in baseball uniforms playing for the town's American Legion team in a few weeks. He had played catch with them several times, and in a couple of informal sandlot games. Stan was a left-handed pitcher with a curve ball, and Jem was a third baseman who might hit for power. They had talked baseball. He began to think about a possible batting order, naming to himself some of the young athletes of the growing town. Then he felt the pressure in the gas nozzle change, and stopped squeezing the handle at exactly the right time, just before the tank was full.

26

The Quadrant

As the first rays of the sun climbed over the mountains, a gray fox was watching the *nopalera* near the miners' tent cabin. She sat curled like a cat beneath the branches of an old creosote, her chin on her paws, a couple of leaps beyond a small monzogranite concavity with a half-inch of water in it. The fox knew that mourning doves and cactus wrens would soon wake, stretch their wings, and emerge from the cholla towards the water.

Her bushy tail twitched with nervous energy, as did her eyes, while she held lax her head, legs, and torso. But she was in the exact spot where other hunters like the roadrunner, coyote, and hawk had lurked before, using the same predator's logic of proximity and concealment. Several of the nested doves, near the perimeter and watchful, knew the fox was there, and their body language alerted the other birds to stay quiet and motionless.

After a few minutes of waiting in vain as the sun climbed, the fox lapped some water and stood at the puddle, gazing into the *nopalera de cholla* with its barbed needles pointing in every direction. Then she lapped more water and swallowed, and paused again for several seconds, relaxed but aware with all her senses. She stretched her haunches and yawned, then exhaled, took a fresh breath and trotted up the hill, around the acacia and mesquite, towards a scrubby plateau known to host cottontail rabbits. One dove, then another, stepped out of the cholla patch near the Anaconda and looked around.

A few minutes later, after the sun had risen above the *nopalera* and lit up the tent cabin, the miners finished their quick, cold breakfast of cornbread and beef jerky. The Captain had a rosy glow to his face, and seemed unusually cheerful for this early hour. As they were sipping the last round from a pot of coffee, he cleared his throat and said, "Gentlemen."

Stan, Jem, and William turned their heads. Haberman was smiling slightly. "This will be the last full day of mining the Anaconda. We're going somewhere new tomorrow, and it might be the place that makes us rich." Each of the three perked their ears or widened their eyes perceptibly. Haberman knew that they were gamblers but not poker players. He continued. "The Anaconda lease goes for another few months. We can keep mining it, and the yields might improve. But I have another stake that could be a thousand times better than this old snake pit." The four of them smiled. "It's been rough going here at the Anaconda, but we're about to turn things around. An old sailor once told me, 'time and tide flow wide.' You fellas have shown yourselves to be square shooters and hard workers, so I'm letting you in on this. It might be the strike of your lives." He looked around at them with a wild-eyed benevolence.

"Is it nearby?" asked William.

"It's several miles south and a couple miles east. Stan has

been there. We can take the truck most of the way, and hike up the wash to the claim. It's on Libélula Peak."

They mulled it over, blinking, not expecting new ideas so early in the morning.

"Captain, if you don't mind a question, has high-grade ore been taken from that claim already?" asked Jem.

"So far, it's just a few nuggets that are like bread crumbs on the doorstep of a bakery. The ore samples have been a little better with every truckful. But I see something there that I rarely see anywhere. Something that will knock your socks off. Have you ever heard about the 'sign of the quartzite four?'" They looked at him blankly. Haberman smiled. "How about the 'four veins junction?'" No reply, and puzzled looks. "It's like the four-leaf clover of mining, gents. But it's not superstition. There's science behind it."

He looked at each of them. William was motionless, looking towards the east, but hearing all the words and sounds. Stan had set his coffee down and was listening intently. Jem looked like he had forgotten the coffee cup in his hand, his thoughts about Alma interrupted by the Captain's remarks. "This is a special situation," continued Haberman. "I'm about to let you in on the secret. I hope you appreciate this, and I need you to show your appreciation by being loyal, by working hard, and by not yapping about this to anyone. Loose lips sink ships. And loose lips make enemies." He looked each of them in the eye with the glare of a hawk or shark. "You with me?" he asked, and each of them assented with a nod and a simple "Yes."

Haberman took a gold coin out of his pocket, flipped it in the air with his thumb, then caught it, slapped it on the back of his palm, and looked at it. "Head's up." He smiled and nodded with an odd twinkle in his eye, put the coin back in his pocket, and continued.

"Let's say you want to follow a vein of quartz down into the monzogranite, hoping it turns into gold, and you see that vein going through rock across the landscape towards the horizon? And maybe you know that sometimes it can join with other veins. But there are places, rare places, where four veins come from four directions to meet, and then run parallel with each other for a short distance. Those places, if you can find them, are the biggest bonanza out there. High-grade gold, almost pure, and in quantity."

Haberman's concept intersected with their own ideas and memories, raising images in their minds. Quine knew the power of four directions, and he had secondhand knowledge of a certain spring that flowed from the ground and then to each of the four compass points, high in the mountains and a sacred place. Jem thought about a rural crossroads of legend where roads came from four directions distant, a place to meet the devil at midnight. Stan was reminded of a nerve center or junction box, where bright veins of quartz and gold might intersect and glow with energy.

"It's time to turn this claim into a working mine. I'm calling it 'Bowline.' Like the knot that you've used a few times lately, the ancient knot from centuries ago, used to tie the bow of a boat to a pier, a dock, or maybe a tree. It's like an anchor, and this new mine will be our anchor, our bowline."

The Captain paused and took a sip of coffee, then continued to speak. "The bowline is a knot that started out doing one thing, but has come to be employed and appreciated for many things. In the same way, you gents started out hammering rock a month ago, then broadened your experience to learn adit and shaft architecture, dynamiting, transporting and milling, the gold market, geology and geometry and some chemistry, small motors and pneumatic drilling, carbide lamps and battery lamps, hard hats and hard heads, ventilation, and probably a few other things that I'm forgetting but might come in handy during the rest of your lives, no matter what you're doing for a living."

He paused again to light his meerschaum pipe, took the first puff of the day, and looked around the circle. He saw that the other three were fully awake and listening, and he continued. "The claim is marked and ripe, and the first leg of the adit is braced, and its entrance offset so that it can't be seen from the main wash." The Captain looked around at them. "Jem and William, you guys work the Anaconda today, get us some low-grade rocks. We'll mix it with Bowline ore so that we don't look too rich too fast. Ryland won't gab, but other people around the mill might."

"When do we get to work the Bowline Mine, Captain, if you don't mind my asking?" inquired Jem.

The Captain replied, "Tomorrow's the day. Stan and I will be leveling the floor and the approach today, and putting in a couple more stulls and beams. See you guys at the tent cabin later tonight."

The gopher snake knew a hundred holes and visited them regularly. He hunted at each opportunity of dawn and sunset, but arrived silently at inexact times and from unexpected angles. The twilight hours were transitory for many species of his potential prey, returning to their burrows or just leaving them. Other animals of interest were also most active at twilight, like rabbits. The snake slithered along a row of gopher and rodent holes under an old concrete slab that once hosted an ore crusher and a two-stamp mill. He peered down a pipe that once brought well water to the mill. There he paused and extended his forked tongue into the air, then quickly retracted it. Then again.

The tongue, working with sensory organs in the roof of his mouth, gave him an acute sense of smell along with other information. Each tine of the forked tongue could sense odors from their relative directions, and the snake's brain compared and combined the data to map an olfactory panorama that highlighted current and recent scents, but included older. He sensed nothing worthwhile in the well pipe, but there were hints of antelope squirrel and kangaroo rat from the south. The snake moved on to the next hole, alertly, quietly, fanged.

<h1 style="text-align:center">27</h1>

The Whiteness of the Whale

At the next daybreak, there was a thunderclap, then a cloudburst. The four miners in their cots woke instantly. A few large raindrops hit the canvas roof with percussive thwacks, but then stopped as the mass of clouds moved onward, obscuring the sunrise. Haberman groaned quietly, then sat on the edge of his cot and peered into the semi-darkness.

"Everyone awake? Must be, after that one." The other three muttered in vaguely affirmative ways, rubbing their eyes and stretching. He continued, "That storm is headed towards Bowline. We might be rained out today." Jem reached for his canteen. Stan stood and stretched. "Be ready to go in a half-hour," said Haberman. "We'll check it out."

On Libélula Peak, a major storm threatened, but only a light rain fell. A pair of mourning doves opened their mouths to the sky. Then they nestled into the sandy hillside, and each lifted a wing to receive the rain. They allowed the rain drops to wash the white down under one wing, then the other. Even the most sparse, irregular rain was welcomed by the doves and all desert dwellers, whether plant, animal, or human. All felt refreshed and renewed.

They convoyed down Utah Trail in the two Fords, with Jem and Quine in one truck, following Haberman and Stan in the other. Haberman was driving, and he looked past Stan towards the west. "Sky looks clear over there. I think we'll have a nice day."

"Gorgonio and Jacinto not brewing any storms?" remarked Stan.

"Sometimes Quail Mountain and Lost Horse Mountain do it too. They snag the rainclouds and hold 'em for a while. Sometimes they'll wring 'em out, and sometimes they'll send us full clouds, but not today," replied Haberman.

"Those clouds at daybreak didn't rain much, but they were large drops."

"Probably nice and cold too. It would have been good to be outside."

Stan smiled. "People in the desert are so happy when it rains. In the city, people never liked it. It slowed down traffic."

"Nothing better than the aroma of a creosote bush after it rains. Fresh and fragrant. Somewhere between pine and mint, but with its own character."

"Sometimes you're downright eloquent, Captain. Did you ever take any college courses in botany, or literature?"

"Never spent a day in college. But I like to read. I dipped into some Eastern philosophy when I was in the Navy. But I was raised on Shakespeare and the King James Bible. That'll give you some words."

"Words, ideas, philosophy, poetry, ethics, religion," replied

Stan.

The road was in good condition, with only a couple shallow puddles in the lowest spots. After a few miles, they turned left onto an old wagon road that had been mostly reclaimed by desert, two inclining tracks that were in some places more interpolated than perceptible.

"Didn't get much rain here either. The storm moved on," said the Captain, nodding towards the east, where dark clouds obscured some of the mountain peaks.

"Looks all clear to drive up to the mine again," replied Stan.

The two vehicles turned off the wagon ruts and went around some boulders, over a dry sand wash that was still dry, along a ridge and around a hill, then upwards adjacent to an alluvial fan at the base of a larger wash that became a canyon higher up the mountain. Haberman turned the truck by grabbing the knob on the steering wheel with his left hand, and then he double-clutched through neutral into reverse and backed into the flat spot nearest the mine. Jem parked his truck in a level area next to a creosote, and then he and William strode briskly up the hill to join Haberman and Stan at the mine. The sun was still behind the clouds, but sparrows were beginning to sing.

"Nice to be working some new ground," remarked Jem.

"Let's see if we can top yesterday's ore. With four of us, we should more than double it," replied the Captain.

Stan reached into the truck bed and picked up a tool bag. "Welcome to the Bowline, gents." Jem and William lifted the air compressor and followed Stan into the tunnel and around the bend, where they placed it near the side wall. Captain Haberman lit a carbide lamp, and hung it on a nail that had been driven into a stull. Then he put their only battery lamp on another nail. Jem placed the gas engine next to the compressor. They quickly connected the two air hoses to pneumatic drills, and fired up the engine and compressor.

On the further leeward side of the mountain, some forty yards away, a tortoise felt the first vibrations of the drilling through the rock strata. He stepped out of his half-moon den in the side of a sand bank, and began the journey downhill to a place where grass might be available for consumption. He grazed there regularly, especially when the grass was green, and it was only a short distance away.

He had located his den on the hillside for safety, but now had the idea to make a secondary burrow, closer to the shaded grassy plain, and less noisy. He listened while he moved. His ability to sense low-pitched sounds and vibrations was sharp enough to pick up the step of a coyote on rock from a few yards away. It was one of his most useful sensory skills, but the vibration of the rock drill made it difficult to hear or feel other things. His senses of smell and direction were now guiding him towards the grass, wet with dew and raindrops in the shadow of the ridge. If threatened by predators, he would rely almost solely on his primary defense, the ability to retract inside his shell, with little help from the secondary defense of vibrational early warning.

Stan relaxed his trigger finger and extracted the pneumatic drill from the granite wall, having reached the target depth of about eight inches. There were a dozen holes honeycombing the rock, most bored with the power drills, but with two drilled more slowly by hand and muscle. He sat the drill against the far wall, and repositioned his goggles to the brim of the helmet.

"Okay, that does it," said the Captain. He reached into a box and began inserting a small stick of dynamite into each socket, making sure each fuse was accessible. "Three each," said the Captain, but they knew that. Each touched three fuses and held them out clear. When the Captain saw that their hands were in position, he lit a match, and so did the others. Each of them lit one, two, three fuses. Jem and Stan each grabbed a lamp, and they all ran down the tunnel, around the bend, and outside. Three of them dashed, and the Captain moved as quickly as he could, directly as a raven might fly.

The twelve sticks exploded and reverberated, most of them simultaneously, and the others within a second's interval. At the same time that the dynamite blew, there was a thunder strike at the top of the mountain, which made them think that they used too much dynamite.

After waiting a few seconds while rocks continued to fall, and then a little longer for most of the dust to settle, the four of them went back into the adit and around the bend, carrying the lamps. What they saw there would change their lives.

What had been a rock wall was in pebbles and shards on the ground, and exposed on the rock face was a diagonal sweep of gold so pure that it glittered in the swaying light of the hand-held lamps.

They stood there for a long moment in awe at the writhen mass of gold that seemed to move and pulse in the light. The Captain spoke first. "Amazing. I've never seen such high-grade gold in this area."

"You say we each own a quarter of this, Captain?" asked Jem.

"You bet. And we're all rich. You'll be rich with what you can stuff in your pockets right now. Let's each grab as many ounces as we can carry, and then later we'll sit down and discuss plans.

We'll need a lockable iron gate at the entrance to this tunnel, and one or two of us should be here at all times, armed. We'll hire guards too."

Captain Haberman moved towards the wall of gold while the others followed his lead, and calmly, as they all noticed. But there was a gleam in their eyes. The Captain almost gently swung a hammer into the wall, and the others used pickaxes and a chisel. The gold was pliable and yielded easily, especially when compared to the granite and quartz they had worked for the past few weeks. The quartz and granite slivers were just blemishes in the bonanza of high-grade gold.

"You were right, Captain. This gold is directly below those four quartz veins," said Stan.

The Captain smiled and spoke softly towards the golden wall as if it were a newborn baby. "The sign of the four. It's all true." They each began pocketing golden nuggets and fragments. Jem dug out a solid chunk of gold that felt like it weighed several pounds. The others whistled at its size, and he put it in the bib pocket of his overalls.

"That one has to be worth a pretty penny. We could live for a year or two on what we'll carry out of here right now," said Stan. Their pockets bulged with newfound wealth. They each dug out gold from various angles with any tool at hand, and marveled at its purity and quantity. Some of it went into the ore bin, but each of them also filled his pockets, sometimes shaking their heads or giving a low whistle in amazement.

Prying and pocketing the gold, William Quine thought of his father, the "wildcat" miner that he had never known. Would he be proud of his son if he could see him now, wealthy with gold, not as a hired hand but part-owner of the mine? He never heard that his father, descended from coal miners, had owned anything, or been able to hold on to anything very long.

William had returned to the desert to learn more about the Native heritage on his mother's side of the family, and rarely thought of his father. But now, he wondered, had he become more like William Quine Sr., the hard-to-know white man who moved from place to place in search of treasure or loot? Then Quine heard an unusual sound from outside the mine.

"Hear that?" he asked. The others became aware of a distant rumble, growing louder.

"Quake!" exclaimed the Captain. "Go!"

They each dropped their tools and ran the twenty yards to the Bowline Mine entrance. Stan and Jem rounded the bend and reached the wash first. The noise sounded like a runaway freight train, then a roaring tornado. Then they looked uphill and saw that it wasn't an earthquake.

The storm, which had moved beyond them to the east, had let loose a deluge on the peak of the mountain and its surrounding slopes, and much of the rainwater from several square miles was drained westward, in their direction, via the rock canyon above them. Smaller canyons drained into this one, and the curly dock from which Jesse had foraged was uprooted. A wall of water came down the slot canyon like it was going down a drain, nine feet tall and accelerating, picking up more sand, rocks, and branches as it gathered force. Yet the sun had climbed above the clouds, and shone through the crest of the wave directly into their mine-darkened eyes. Stan and Jem tried to climb the sheer sidewalls of the canyon, but there was very little foothold for their month-old, thick-soled, steel-toed boots, which glittered with gold, and their pockets seemed to weigh them down.

"Fourteen times heavier than sand," thought Jem, remembering Izzy's words about the relative weight of gold. Stan knew in a split-second of hindsight what had happened, and why he hadn't expected it, growing up in a flatland where a stormfront would do no damage after it had passed. He suddenly felt very thirsty, but with an odd clarity and calm.

Quine hung back to help the Captain, and they reached the wash very quickly. But the wall of water loomed. The Captain tasted brine at the back of his throat, and felt the spray of the tide. He saw the frothy white mass at the torrent's leading edge, what the old-timers called "the snout" of the flood, and to him it was a reckoning leviathan with familiar features: a white head, a wrinkled brow, and a crooked jaw. *"The Whale,"* he said to himself, with recognition and finality.

Looking up at the flood, Quine in his last moment relived his life in a flash, moving back through work and at sea and in school and in foster homes, and in a dormitory, then in a horse-drawn wagon, then a small adobe house. Then he was in the white quartz cave from his repeated dreams, and he was walking from the back of the cave as before. He walked around the people sitting on ledges and on the floor, and they looked up and smiled. He recognized them as kindred, the extended family of Serrano and Chemehuevi from his mother's side. His people. Though he never spent time with them after his early childhood, now they knew him, and looked at him with affection. He was a beloved family member who belonged with them, here and now. His grandfather was in a place of honor, looking at him with a complicated expression, then smiling.

In his vision, he walked up to the entrance of the cave, and saw that the family's attention had been focused on a small grotto with privacy in its concavity, around the corner from the quartz chamber. Four women were gathered there, attending to another woman inside. As he moved closer, a couple of them smiled and gestured, and made room for him to come closer. Then he saw that the other woman was in labor, and he recognized and remembered this place as the childbirth cave, the sacred chamber where life began for many of the area's Natives. The woman in labor had her eyes closed in pain and concentration, but then she opened them and looked at Quine, and he saw that it was his own mother. He saw her love for him, and he knew that she hadn't given him up voluntarily. He returned her love with his gaze. Then he looked down and saw that the baby had emerged and was being cradled by one of the women. He looked at the newborn, and strangely, the baby opened his eyes, and when their eyes met, William Quine saw himself. That was the last thing he saw.

Postscript

The clouds detached from the atmosphere of the mountain peak, and drifted to the east. The sky cleared. The sun rose over the Pintos, and then the Hexie and Queen mountains, and began to illuminate facets of the mountains on three sides, with shadows to the north. The rocky plateaus and crags began to absorb and then radiate heat. The patches with trees, bushes, grasses, and wildflowers were cooler than the rocky areas. By late morning, the difference in surface temperatures created columns of rising air above the gneiss, monzogranite, and quartz. Some raptors used these updrafts to soar and spiral to a higher level, without flapping their wings or otherwise expending much energy. Like an ore mill, or more like a roller coaster using a conveyor belt to reach a summit, these raptors would repeatedly grab the thermal updraft with their spread wings, then swerve and swoop with gravity to lower altitudes.

Gliding from warm currents into cooler air, then dipping a wing to turn, a turkey vulture narrowed his gyre. He scrutinized a rivulet that had gushed down the mountainside after the storm, eying the flotsam. Along with branches and boulders and thick muddy sand, there would be fresh carrion, the drowned corpses of rodents and jackrabbits and maybe larger mammals. Soon he was joined by another vulture. They focused on the perimeter of the alluvial fan at the base of the mountain, where the rushing water would diffuse over a larger area, and the carrion would eventually come to rest. They had experienced a rainwater bonanza in this spot twice in the last few years. But this flood was more propulsive and violent, which seemed promising.

They frequently were drawn to carrion by its odor of decomposition, but that odor would bring other turkey vultures to the area. If they could spot their targets visually, before the rot escalated in redolence, they would have the first choice of prime cuts. Unlike most predators, who were drawn to moving prey, the turkey vultures only ate corpses, which in most cases were stationary. But motion, especially the erratic and unusual, would draw their attention. The vultures would watch closely any creatures that seemed out of place in the mountains, and they were vigilant to the potential of carnage in various situations including weather.

As they each dipped a wing into a slow arc of focus, the vultures saw a human body float down the rivulet and crash against boulders, catch on a branch, then break free and float some more. They saw another body carried by downhill currents, twisted and broken. Then there were two more, with arms and legs oddly akimbo. The vultures glided and dropped to where the bodies would skid to rest at the edge of the alluvium.

"You're watering now?" asked Lee.

"Sure am," replied Alma. "We haven't got any rain yet, and probably won't." She held the water can in the crook of her arm, and carefully sprinkled well water onto tomato and cucumber plants. The raised bed was protected by a dome of chicken wire, and a nearby scarecrow with cactus hands.

Lee glanced up at the sky and its gray, slow-moving clouds. "You're probably right. The clouds just pass on by."

"But the plants feel what's in the air, and they open their stomata. They're expecting water, so I'll give 'em some," said Alma.

"See, that's why you have a green thumb. You think about things from the plants' point of view."

"You could probably paint that sky, and it would be good. But I can tell you're not going to, because you're not looking at it very hard."

Lee chuckled. "You change the subject every time someone compliments you. But you're right about that. I don't paint stormy skies very much."

"You should have seen the lightning to the south. They probably got a nice rain in the mountains down there."

"Lucky them! Maybe some of the cacti will open their flowers, and I'll paint them. Under a blue sky," said Lee.

Standing upright on his hind legs, a jackrabbit chews on a creosote leaf. He samples the new growth at the fringes, preferring the smaller leaves that are vibrantly green, crisp, and aromatic. Like many desert animals, and some desert humans, he nibbles on creosote every now and then. A leaf or two has a tonic, invigorating quality. It is not the bulk of his diet, but a regular supplement. The desert iguana also likes an occasional leaf, and enjoys chewing the yellow blossoms that flutter to the ground after a summer rain.

Hummingbirds, bats, bees, and flies are also drawn to the creosote's golden blossoms, where they sip nectar and pollinate liberally. After pollination, a blossom's petals will rotate inward a quarter-turn, and the flower will appear more like a pinwheel than a lush, receptive floral vulva. A hovering pollinator will notice the difference, and move on to a different flower. After some weeks, the flowers become fuzzy seed balls, a few of which are used and distributed by birds and rodents to cushion and insulate their nests.

Over the centuries, humans have also recognized the creosote for a multitude of uses, and its tonic, healing, and antiseptic properties. If you scrub a stone *mortero* with a creosote sprig, then brush away the crushed green leaves with some coiled-up fibers from a yucca leaf, the *mortero* will be clean, and then cleaner still if you dowse it with water that has been boiled over a fire. The *mortero* will be sanitized and ready to grind seeds into flour, crush leaves into medicine, and activate herbs to ease the pain of childbirth, among other uses.

Tiny seeds from other plants and flowers are carried by the wind to the gathering arms of the creosote, and they pepper the ground below its shady canopy. Seeds from other plants will not grow there, deterred by the creosote's subtle resinous secretions. The windblown seeds are browsed and foraged by quail, doves, sparrows, and many other birds, as well as rabbits and squirrels. Some call the creosote *"La Gobernadora,"* the governess, and the outspread branches of the mature creosote offer protection and nourishment to many desert animals. When a hawk or falcon appears, the mourning doves will sound their whistling wings of alarm, and songbirds, quail, squirrels, and rabbits will run to the safety of the governess and her green canopy.

Coveys of chattering quail dash from one creosote to another for much of the day, voicing happy squeaks of discovery and camaraderie, eating tiny seeds and bits of foliage off the ground again and again. When they are in open sand between bushes and trees, vulnerable to predators, they more than double their walking speed until they reach the shade and safety of the next creosote, where they relax, eat, and socialize together. They can fly when necessary, but walking uses less energy.

But the next bush, which appears to be a separate plant, is connected to the others by a crown root, which encircles the tap roots of each creosote in a ring. Like the eight arms of an octopus, a ring of eight creosotes might represent the appendages of a single being. The crown root can store moisture and nutrients to be shared by each bush in the ring. What seem to be separate organisms are connected in unseen and ancient ways.

Not always clustering in circles, creosotes sometimes line up as rectangles, triangles, polygons, or glyphs. They may root their connection in abstruse combination, in shapes that seem obscure and random to us, yet were fully formed, for their own reasons, centuries before the most rudimentary powers of human discernment evolved in the minds of our young species. Some creosote rings are more than ten thousand years old, among the oldest living things on the planet, and the species is far older.

For a thousand centuries and more, the unique fragrance of the creosote has wafted through the desert after a rain. For some recent fraction of those thousand centuries, humans who live in the American deserts have inhaled and welcomed that refreshing aroma.

After the rain, a creosote leaf or two is especially tasty to the jackrabbit, who can survive for weeks without liquid water if necessary, taking moisture from foliage. In addition to the other root systems, the creosote has a network of tendrils near the surface, reaching out beyond the shade canopy like slender capillaries to absorb water from even slight rains, and dispatching that moisture to the leaves quickly. The jackrabbit enjoys the taste of the moist, fragrant leaves, in moderation, and enjoys the droplets of water that bead on their protective waxy surface. Every living thing is pleased when it rains in the desert, and the gladness wafts through the fresh desert air with the aroma of creosote.

On a slack afternoon at the American Legion, veteran Bob Correy and veteran Jesse Palmer, the retired blacksmith, sat at a card table drinking iced tea and making remarks about stories in the week-old newspapers. They noticed a tall young stranger in a Stetson hat looking at the bulletin board, and writing something on a piece of cardboard.

"Another argonaut for the dusty shafts," observed Jesse.

"Another argonaut's gonna get fleeced," replied Bob.

A small man with a large mustache was sitting at the bar, sipping coffee, watching the room in the mirror behind the bottle rack. He had also noticed the cowboy, and then extinguished his cigar and sidled over to the newcomer.

"Good opportunities 'round here," he said to the cowboy.

"A lot going on," replied the cowboy.

"You looking to get into mining?"

"Well, maybe."

"Ever considered vermiculite?"

"Not particularly. I'm interested in gold mining."

"Funny you should say that. I have a line on a couple excellent claims. An energetic young man with a partner or a crew could do very well. What's your name?"

"J.P. Robusto. Good to meet you." They shook hands.

"Call me Izzy."

Between one full moon and the next, the Joshua flowers have folded inwards and transformed themselves into oval fruits. Each fruit contains round, flat seeds that are stacked like discs and arrayed in six rows around a center, corresponding to the six sepals that formed the flower's calyx. The fruits will dry and drop to the ground by fall, but now they hold strong to their stems, even in a brisk wind. The yucca larvae have eaten several of the seeds, but never all of them, and usually less than half.

The larvae, in the form of tiny caterpillars that range from pale to pink to orange in color, chew their way out of the fruit, making tiny holes that look like pin-pricks in the husks. Frequently this happens after a rainfall. Today, the tiny caterpillars will fall to the ground and burrow several inches into the moist sand, where they will spin cocoons that will protect them as they sleep and metamorphose through summer and winter into next spring, or maybe the one after that, when they will emerge as adult moths, and the cycle begins again. The yucca moths will mate in the moonlight, and the females will find Joshua blossoms in which to lay their eggs. Then the female moths will pollinate the flowers, not accidentally or incidentally, but with specific intention. The mutual interdependence of the yucca moths and Joshua trees will bear fruit again.